stay with me

stay with me

Hanne Ørstavik

Translated from the Norwegian by Martin Aitken

SHEFFIELD – LONDON – NEW YORK

First published in English in the UK in 2024 by And Other Stories
Sheffield – London – New York
www.andotherstories.org

First published as *Bli hos meg* by Forlaget Oktober AS, 2023
Published in agreement with Oslo Literary Agency

1 3 5 7 9 8 6 4 2

ISBN: 9781916751088
eBook ISBN: 9781916751095

Editor: Stefan Tobler; Copy-editor: Madeleine Rogers; Proofreader: Gesche Ipsen; Typesetter: Tetragon, London; Typefaces: Albertan Pro and Linotype Syntax (interior) and Stellage (cover); Series Cover Design: Elisa von Randow, Alles Blau Studio, Brazil, after a concept by And Other Stories; Author Photo: Baard Henriksen.

And Other Stories books are printed and bound in the UK on FSC-certified paper by the CPI Group (UK) Ltd, Croydon. The covers are of 299gsm Vanguard card, containing a minimum of 30% upcycled fibre, and are made in the Lake District at the environmentally friendly James Cropper paper mill. They are embossed with biodegradable foils.

A catalogue record for this book is available from the British Library.

And Other Stories gratefully acknowledge that our work is supported using public funding by Arts Council England.

This translation has been published with the financial support of NORLA.

//

No one at home ever said they loved me. If I'd asked, I know they would have said yes, Mamma and Pappa, of course they loved me. Only I didn't ask, part of the reason being that I didn't want Pappa getting angry. And of course it was such an unquestionable thing. Like God loving mankind. It's something you know. Why couldn't I feel it?

They never touched each other, caresses, there was no tenderness between them. Mamma thought Pappa was sentimental, pathetic, pitiful, and at the same time she was afraid of him, afraid to death, there'd been that business with the axe out in the fields in the snow, in the middle of the night, Pappa had been drinking home-made vodka (so Mamma said), he went mad, ran wild and jumped over the stone wall, I can see it in my mind's eye, over the wall in one leap, in the snow, so young and strong and lithe he must have been then, Pappa, younger than M is now, thirty-three or thirty-four, but now Pappa tells me it wasn't like that at all, he hadn't touched a drop, and he hadn't gone mad either, the axe part had been misunderstood, he hadn't been going for anyone but had taken the axe with him to use as a gavel, like in court, to emphasise something, a standpoint, most likely they'd been talking politics, your father's gone mad, he's gone running after people with an axe, and it all ended with the vet injecting him with a sedative, it took several men to bring him down and keep him there. But the thing with the axe is such a long time ago now, Mamma was pregnant with me when it happened, and it was only the once. It wasn't Pappa with an axe we were afraid of. We were just afraid. What was it we were so afraid of?

It had to do with love, with the word being taken so much for granted I couldn't feel anything. The only thing I could feel was afraid, afraid was real, the whole time. I can't remember how it would happen, that Pappa would get angry. It just did. You could knock a glass over or be late for dinner. Your boot could have chafed your ankle while you were up on the fell, so you needed a plaster. You could get a fishing lure stuck after a cast. Perhaps you'd scribbled on the pad by the telephone. Or a school friend might come and ring the doorbell while we were having our dinner. It wasn't these things in themselves, it was what they stood for: not being thoughtful enough, not being heedful. It wasn't leaving the milk out, it was being *that sort of person*. The sort who's negligent, thoughtless, who never pays heed. It seems like such a small thing when I write it down. But it wasn't small, it was everything. The world was hard. Wrong was wrong. When it could have been right. Afraid was a state of being. I don't know when it started. All I know is that I was afraid, afraid was a skin beneath my skin that couldn't be shed.

It's strange to be writing this. That we were afraid. It makes me cry, I'm crying now as I write, I'm saying out loud to myself: afraid was all we were. We were afraid the whole time. Now I'm nearly fifty-three years old.

And I ask myself – what were we supposed to have been if we hadn't been afraid? It's almost as if there's something missing, something else to have been instead. That too seems strange as I write it down, but it's what I'm thinking: if we hadn't been scared, if being scared had suddenly stopped, what would we have been instead?

When fear has become one's inner layer, the part of you that's real. If that's then taken away: what's left is like an enormous crater. Fear is total. Fear is water coming in everywhere, in every nook and cranny, under every bed. The girl I was, when she was ten for instance, if the fear she knew, if the reason for that fear, the most obvious reason, Pappa, hadn't been there any more, if Pappa had died or Mamma had left him and taken me with her, would I not have been afraid any more? What would I have been then? Who am I, when I'm not afraid?

There's something more. There's something that can't be traced back to a single point – it's not like that. It's something else, and I don't know what it is.

I just didn't understand. You can see it in the photos from when I was little. We were at the photographer's in Vadsø when I was two, black and white, shades of grey, I'm sitting on Pappa's knee, in a dark pleated skirt and white tights, my brother a year older on Mamma's knee beside us. The others are smiling, but not me, I look scrutinous. It's like I'm struggling to understand, the whole time. What are we doing? What are we doing here? I think I just didn't get the point of anything the whole time I was growing up. Why live, if there's no joy? If life isn't good, if there's no softness to it, if there's no – love?

And, at the same time, feeling left out. Love was something others were doing. I saw it in films and could imitate it. But it wouldn't let me in. I had no idea how to do it, felt ashamed of myself for the same reason. I tried to hide it. It just wouldn't happen for me.

So when my husband, the father of our daughter, said, after twelve years, that there were other ways of living with a person, ways that were more loving, I knew he was right. I couldn't do it. We got divorced. Because knowing never helped. I've known it all along. I've just never known what to do about it.

Ten years ago I met L, a publisher, and with L being close to someone became something good. What do I mean by that? I mean that slowly – sometimes yes, sometimes not – I began to loosen up and accept the presence in my life of another person. He was so kind. Gentle. His soft olive skin. The way his goodness shimmered in him, the way it could be seen in his face, his eyes, his little tremble. His hand, dry and warm. He asked nothing of me that I didn't have. He made me feel, again and again, that I was good enough, better than I often thought. That I was welcome, and that he wanted me the way I was.

Four years it lasted, during the last two L was ill, and then he died. That's two years ago now. A year later I met M. But even before L died, I knew I was going to write this novel. I've known it was there, I just never got started, I've waited and waited for it to open itself out to me and take me in, I've waited like mad for it to start happening.

//

The first thing I wrote, even before L died, was this:

She kneels and looks down into the water. A floating jetty extends some distance, it could have been a bridge, only it stops. Where it stops is where she kneels.

She looks down into the water, as if the water was a membrane and there was another world underneath.

As if what's there, in that other world, is bits of her, bits that aren't visible to her, or to anyone.

And so she kneels and looks down into the water, and it's not that she's waiting, she's just being.

For a couple of years, only that image. I got no further. And it's true, she wasn't waiting. She was being. Being there on the jetty, being that image inside me, a state of being. It's me who's been waiting. Going around with that image, standing on the shore, walking all the way out along the jetty behind her, sitting down next to her, trying to see what she sees. Only I've never been able to reach her, have seen nothing.

And then one day it becomes possible to write:

She has remained there. She came with Myrto who was conducting at the concert hall, only then he died.

They'd been married just over a year, known each other five. She buried his ashes under the tree in front of the house, the one she sees from the window when she looks out. Last week his daughter told her she wanted some of his ashes too, to spread them somewhere (Papà). Judith scraped the grit aside with a trowel and there underneath lay the ashes still, as if a whole autumn of rain and a winter of snow had not passed since she buried them there, piles of snow that froze and later melted, over and over, and she tipped some of the ashes into a small container made of metal and sent them by post across the sea.

The images are so still. Unmoving. As if they've simply stopped. *She being is all there is.* But what is she? She is this body that exists through the days. When night comes she lies down in the big bed, on the mattress that's too soft, she turns off the light and the night is then all around her until it's morning again.

A short time he was with her. In the mornings when they woke, he would look at her from his pillow and his grey eyes were so soft upon her.

Afterwards, in the beginning, she cried from the pit of her stomach, a weeping that was heavy and felt endless, that she could go in and out of, that was there with her the whole time.

How long does the beginning last. When does the beginning melt into something else, and become a person's days. And when do those days change, and become something else still.

And what is there now? It's as if she has emerged from what was dark and oppressive and hung over her, into something wide open and empty.

It's not possible to know more about her than this. We see what we see. She knows no more about herself.

There are no eyes any more that see her as he saw her. That see in such a way that she could feel waves surging from a point in her middle, the heart presumably, as if her heart was a pink and opening bud agitating the surface of a bright green lake, bringing its waters into motion.

She had never been there before, to it lasting. To the softness in her chest enduring. To it not being cut off, the goodness in his eyes, that made it happen. To it not suddenly being gone. She started to believe in it, to bend, and become without thought.

And then it was he who was gone.

They were picked up at the airport by the concert hall's factotum. They had two big suitcases each, Myrto's two red ones and hers, a black and a blue. Her hand luggage included her laptop, the old heavy one, and a few books she hadn't been able to leave behind. There'd been no logic to her choice, she'd simply taken the ones that had stood out to her as she scanned the bookshelves back home in Milan. Besides his sheet music, Myrto had with him a collection of Chekhov's short stories and two books in French about music and meaning, as well as the notebook in which he wrote things down in tiny handwriting. It had always bemused her how a hand that could write so small could also make so much sound happen – how his body, so soft and gentle next to hers, could contain the same man who would burst into such life in front of an orchestra. So wild he appeared then, so unfamiliar and unexplored. The way she often thought of him when he came inside her, that every thrust was him, straining for the very limits, for insecurity and frailty too, straining for where there was no longer any distance between what was inside him and what was outside, in the music. And she had her first dress with her too, the one she'd sewn in secondary school, the fabric was brown, cotton, she'd sat in the kitchen with the sewing machine on the wobbly table, the evenings grew lighter with each day and when at last she was finished she'd worn it one day at school, only it hadn't been at all like she'd imagined, that something about her would be made visible, that the dress would open something, draw the others closer to her, instead it was the opposite that happened, it was as if they moved still further away, she saw how they tried to hide their sniggers, no one understood, and yet the dress had survived, she took it with her every time she moved somewhere new.

In the car on their way from the airport Myrto engaged in chat with Hardy, as the driver was called, while Judith looked out of the window, and even then: the feeling of everything being too big. That she'd ended up in a world where everything was oversized, the streets were extra wide, the buildings extra tall. As if everything was so big she could see the curvature of the earth, like on a beach where the whole horizon stretches out in front of you, the way it tilts away at the edges.

And the way she'd felt immediately that the green timber house in front of which Hardy pulled up was a place to be glad for, a home. It was a semi, theirs was on the right, two floors, red and yellow around the windows, it made her think of Pippi Longstocking. The other half, identical, was empty when they arrived, and still is now. The house belongs to the philharmonic and the concert hall. Hardy gave them the keys and wished them welcome, turned and waved as he went back to the car, and they stood a moment on the porch with their suitcases before unlocking the door and going inside.

Myrto holds the front door open for her as she steps through into the big hallway where the first thing she notices is the staircase, its brown hemp runner secured by a polished brass rod on every stair. He follows her in and pauses, his fawn-coloured coat hanging open, his tousled hair swept back from his face as if he's been standing in a strong wind, and he smiles, yes, he smiles at her.

And in that image of him smiling there, in the hallway of the house in which they're going to live, she sees glimpses of so many other moments, she sees him in the music room in Milan, where the piano was, and the keyboard with the headphones, the big iMac on the desk beside it where he wrote his music, and in those moments he is so very far inside himself, or what he is listening to, or doing, standing shaking his arms that are held out at his sides, his eyes closed, or else he's seated at the piano and looks so small, as if the piano is enormous and he's just a little boy sitting on the stool, stretching up to reach, his back quite straight and his nose as pointed as a bird's beak, stretching towards the sheet music higher up.

The way she's closest to him when he's not thinking that she's there too, when he's doing what he does and is not only immersed but consumed, it's the intensity in him then that opens him to her, something opens to show her the place inside him that is so alive, and when he smiles at her in the hallway in the green house, she sees that place inside his smile.

Further inside, everything is so big, the worktop in the kitchen, like the ones she's seen in films, in the middle of the floor, *The Bridges of Madison County*, Meryl Streep a fifties housewife, Clint Eastwood constantly pulling up outside in his pickup, he's a photographer and from the Midwest, from Bellingham, Minnesota, not far from where they are now, and Francesca, as Meryl's character is called, is Italian, and now she and Myrto coming straight from Milan, as if there's a connection, Judith thinks, standing there in the kitchen, but says nothing, simply watches Myrto as if he was Clint and she was Streep, and now it's all about *them*, the two of them together, in the kitchen, where the sink stands in front of a wide bay window. Now we're in *America*, she thinks as she opens the extra-wide fridge. The 2.5-litre plastic bottle of milk, the brown paper bags on the worktop with the groceries someone's bought for them at the supermarket. The big sofa, also green, in front of the fireplace, a blanket with stars and stripes draped over the armrest.

And there, inside the door, Myrto lifts her up in his unmuscular arms, strong enough nonetheless, and staggers the few steps to the staircase, and they laugh, she buries her nose in his white hair and sniffs in his smell, his hair, thinning now on top, revealing to her the brown flecks on the pink of his scalp, here a strand, there a strand, like stems of trees in a vast forest in which she's running about – *Myrto*, she says, and pulls his head to her chest, the globe of the earth and the heavens together, and now she holds the whole world in her hands.

And then he had to go and DIE? It's impossible to even imagine then. No one goes around thinking about death like that, Judith tells herself afterwards, by which point she thinks about death all the time, she sees it in her own face, Hello death, she says to the wrinkles around her mouth, to the skin that sags beneath her chin, Hello there, and death is then no longer unfamiliar, death is the inside of her hand as she smooths a length of fabric that will be made into a dress that will be draped upon her body that will one day die, it too, yes, the body inside the dress will die, and this gives everything a strange lightness, Judith thinks, that this is how it is, that everything is dead too.

//

The city lies on both sides of a big river, grown together, an amalgamation of two cities, the green house at 297 Dayton Avenue in the part of the city that's called St. Paul. The river is the Mississippi, there are lakes all around, and further away from the city is the prairie, Native American land, the signage in the city centre is in both American and Ojibwe. Minneapolis. The name apparently means *the two settlements by the river*, but to Judith's mind it conjures up Heraklion, Neapolis, towns of long ago submerged now for hundreds of years under the sea, though this is the American Midwest, there's no sea here, not anywhere.

She knows what infatuation feels like, an effervescence. But that other thing, fondness, to love another person, is something she doesn't know where to look for in herself. How could she have known what he meant when he said how much he was fond of her? Would it go on, would it last, would he still be there when day came round again?

I am Judith, I live in the green house at 297 Dayton Avenue, I am Norwegian and was married in Italy, and when we came to America he died. She says the words in front of the mirror in the hallway, behind her she sees the sturdy banister of the staircase, the wood worn smooth, its grand swirl at the bottom, like a big seashell. I am fifty-two years old. I am a widow, she says, and looks into her own eyes. It makes no impression. It happened the way it happened, and everything has led to this, here, now.

Now it's about what *isn't* here, she thinks. I am Judith, I live in the green house, I am fifty-two years old and he isn't coming back. He won't be coming in through the door this afternoon to rest before the evening's performance, but when he still did they would sometimes lie on the sofa together, at each end, so they could look at each other, or they would just lie there with their eyes closed and not say anything, but sense and savour there being such fullness and such quietness, as if they were being held by something soft, as if they were lying in a little blue rowing boat that was rocking them both.

She is surprised by her recollection, the way it's so together, so restful and reassuring, because she knows it wasn't like that, not then. Then it was the uncertainty, the whole time, of whether he actually wanted her. Was it real? He could meet someone else, discard her.

Myrto was angry once. Judith wouldn't have thought he had such anger in him. But he did.

It was her birthday, their first after they'd met, and they'd woken up together in his family's house by the sea, the solid house his father had purchased after Myrto had come of age, and it was where he died, Myrto's father. It was the only night they ever spent in the house, which was designed by a well-known architect and stood high up on a hillside with vistas of the bay and the small islands off the coast, there they had woken up, and it could have been so nice, it could have been wonderful, only it wasn't, because Myrto couldn't stand being in that house and all he wanted was to be somewhere else, to go back home. They woke up and he didn't mention it, she told herself it wasn't important, but he did nothing to acknowledge it, he could have bought a little cake from the bakery on the corner when they went to get the bus to the railway station, but there was no present, no card, no nothing. It deflated her. She didn't mention it all day, not until they got home, when they got in and took off their shoes and were home.

She can't remember what she said, something to the effect maybe that she found it strange that it meant so little, her birthday. That was all. But he hit the roof. His face contracted like it was made of rubber, he coiled his body and yelled, and threw something at her that skidded across the floor, she can't remember what. He was completely distorted in front of her eyes. He was someone else, he wasn't Myrto any more, there was something else inside him, a raging rubber beast, he was out of control, and Judith can't remember herself being afraid, although she thinks she must have been, all she knows is that she remembers it so clearly, so vividly. And that it altered something. It was as if she realised then that he wasn't whole and strong, the way she'd thought, but that there was something weak in him, there was a point inside him where nothing could hold, and after that day, that birthday, that point was a place she tried to avoid.

She has avoided it in her thoughts as well, has not dwelled on his anger but has looked the other way, left it there in the edgeland and gone back to everything else, nourishing instead the softness, the mildness, the kindness, the tenderness, that vast place in his eyes from which she would never be turned away.

Where are you? She's standing in the hallway and sees him step towards the front door, on the other side of it, outside.

She looks into the mirror. The big mirror, on top of a console table with curved legs. Everything is so quiet.

He won't be coming in again, not ever. She looks into the eyes in the mirror and says the words once more. The woman in the mirror seems not to hear. Judith looks at herself and thinks: So alone you look. If it was someone she knew, she would hold her tight and stroke her hair. But with this one in the mirror she can't.

11

Since Judith buried his ashes under the tree, the birds have been coming there. Perhaps they did before, without her noticing. But she sees them now. She sits on the decking, the covered veranda, it's as if the house were a great ship, a blanket over her knees, another around her shoulders – there's a bench there, like the ones they have in parks and other public places, and she's brought a chair out from inside to rest her legs on. She sits there now that spring has come, and watches the birds.

She knows nothing about birds, but has dug out a booklet from the bookshelf next to the fireplace, *Our Most Common Backyard Birds*, a local publication, so now she uses the English names, *robin*, *crow*, sometimes *cardinal* or *blue jay*. Some others are called *chickadees*. And of course there are sparrows, lots of small sparrows. They're the ones that make her think about Myrto the most, the little ones. A squirrel lives close by too, often she'll see it dart up a tree or busying about among the branches and leaves, doing whatever it does, she has no idea, but its earnest activity makes her smile – imagine a life like that, filled by a single purpose, the body working only in accordance with that, and not a single muscle or thought, not a doubt, to pull you in any other direction or cause you to stop.

She's been making things, or rather not *things*, clothes, or not *clothes* exactly either, because what are clothes anyway, clothes aren't ever just clothes, everything's an expression of something, a choice, or is it? I write this about Judith and think of the Roma boys at the children's home in Romania where I worked as a volunteer one summer when I was a student, just after the country opened up, the boys there had nothing of their own, no possessions of any sort, nothing that was theirs and theirs alone, save perhaps for their bodies, if they were lucky and none of the men or the older boys availed themselves, and whenever they got dressed they'd have to rummage through the pile on the floor of the laundry room to see if they could find something their size and then put it on as quickly as they could before someone else came and claimed it, a pair of trousers or whatever, and for a few days they were their trousers, until everything got washed again and they'd have to repeat the process, finding something that fitted, in the big pile on the laundry-room floor. So perhaps, like so many other things, like the Roma boys having to make do as best they could in poverty, Judith making clothes, costumes, wasn't simply a choice, but also a question of money. Judith isn't poor. She's not wealthy either, but she is Norwegian and occasionally the recipient of a grant, and for periods at a time she has worked on some large-scale productions. Sometimes she worked at the opera house, in the costume department, it was how she met Myrto, when he was working in Oslo, and she continued living the same way when she went with him to Italy, she rented a workspace in a sewing workshop and had her machine there and would sit in the evenings with her lamp shining on the fabric that spilled over the table like the wake of a fishing boat trailing into the great darkness, the needle whirring without cessation, to release its trawl.

And all the time, inside everything, underneath everything: the fear that he wasn't really, not really committed. Committed to her. She would come home late, after working all evening, open the door, enter the living room, and he'd be sitting at one end of the sofa with a book, earphones, and he would turn his head and look up, and smile. But she, always: seconds before his eyes met hers: not knowing: not knowing if it was still there. The whole time expecting it to be gone, that soft place, no longer there for her.

Like that place was the only thing she needed.

Her sewing machine is in the front room on the first floor, the one above the bay window, there was an octagonal table already there when they moved in and she's been sitting at it with an extension lead plugged into the wall. Now, thinking about her sewing machine, sewing, all she sees is Myrto in the open coffin, already diminished, in his dark suit and pink tie, pink with a pattern of yellow circles, he never wore a tie, but she knew that he too would consider the white shirt to be lacking without one, too sorry-looking, pathetic, and then all the polyester by which he was surrounded, a shiny yellow-beige hollow in which he lay as if in a canoe, the same smooth fabric she would see again when his ashes were later delivered to her, a metal container in a bag made of the same fabric, embroidered with the City of Minneapolis emblem and with drawstrings – it was pretending to be silk, only it wasn't.

And now it's the birds that are shiny, Judith thinks to herself as she sits on the bench, like the tail of the blue jay, she sees one perched on a slender branch halfway up the tree, the grey-blue plumage, the tail, that will not be stilled but wags towards the light, a completely different blue, tinged with yellow verging on green, more like the sea, which anyway is its hope, that there will be something else, something more.

One time in Milan she made him a caftan, a coat, a full-length garment in heavy, bright material with bands of different coloured fabrics running up the middle and down the back, coarse and shiny, with snatches of purple brocade. She helped him put it on, the sleeves were wide and when he held out his arms they looked like wings.

The way everything is so big and there's no movement anywhere. As if she's a little girl in an over-dimensioned house surrounded by streets and trees and enormous skyscrapers, the big river rushing its course, and all around, to all sides, the endless prairie. The path leading across the lawns, and there's such a long way to the cars and to the outside walls of the house. Space between all things.

//

Sitting at a desk in the reading room at the Deichman, the way I'd sit thirty years ago at Blindern when I was a sociology student. I remember where I was then, because of the other students, because of the sounds, I wore earplugs and would always sit at the end of a row, by the window or the wall. But now I'm sitting in the middle, at a long, high desk with tall stools to sit on, green plants on the wall, two girls sitting next to me, they're listening to music, an earphone each inside their black hijabs, heads together, I can hear the bass and the treble. I always liked working from home the best. Now all I want is not to be there – the living room's too quiet, the snow's too quiet, the grey sky. I have with me my laptop and my notebook, and the book I'm reading. The important thing is not how much I get done, but being here. Sitting in the soft light of the work stations, seeing other human bodies and not being on my own any more.

I'm in Oslo for a week, it's my publisher's fiftieth birthday, and nearly every night, as often as I can, I go to see Pappa in the yellow flats at the top of Kirkeveien, I go up the stairs and inside, and there are the pictures he's painted, hanging on the walls or stacked up against them, still lifes, copies of classics, and other paintings done from photographs for practice, his children too when we were little, the brothers, one of me with the doll I had, I'm holding her in my lap, Victoria. Pappa will be eighty-seven this summer and has trouble with his oesophagus, he has good days, but then bad days, too, when he can barely breathe and coughs up mucus that he spits out into a serviette, sometimes when he coughs like that and wheezes for air it can seem like it's the end, but that's the way it's been for years now and he doesn't want us to make a fuss, so I sit down next to him on the sofa in front of the TV and pretend not to notice. His hearing isn't impaired, but he has the sound turned up loud, it comes across as a form of respect, we're watching the news from Ukraine, the Russian invasion, first we watch NRK, then SVT, then the BBC, we watch the images from the bombed housing blocks, people moving about below the blackened holes where the windows once were, with their suitcases and duvets, the Ukrainian president speaking from a gilded chair in his green T-shirt, It reminds me of the planes, Pappa says, when he was a small boy in Ørsta and the German bombers would come in low from behind the great Sunnmørsalpene mountain range, and he coughs and wheezes, You wouldn't hear them coming because of the mountains, Pappa says, then all of a sudden they'd be there.

Dark outside. The fjord dark, the dark lump of Hovedøya.

The hijab girls have put their phones down, the earphones too, though the music's still running, and now they've opened their workbooks, they've got pencils and highlighters, pink, yellow and green, they highlight this, they highlight that, after a while there's hardly anything left that hasn't been highlighted, as if they're trying to bring everything up onto another level, I think to myself, to turn it into something more, to make the pages as decorative as possible, regardless of what's written on them.

I look at the screen as if there was an opening in it through which I could crawl and then sit down inside, lean back against a wall and look at what was around me, and what I would see then, in there, would be the novel, everything it had to do and wanted to do. But there is no opening, no way in, anywhere.

Selby Avenue, Summit Avenue, Laurel Avenue and Ashland. These are the streets around Dayton.

It feels like such an endless expanse to take on, the great prairie, the wars, Silver Arrow and Moonbeam, the feather headdresses we once had, my brothers and me, when we played in the heather among the saplings of birch at Tana Bru. I think about it when writing about Judith as she stands on the bridge over the great rushing river in Minneapolis. That it's like having entered another stage of my own childhood, Judith going around in something that has the same form, only everything's much bigger.

When I was a little girl, and then fourteen, fifteen, I remember a sense of expectation, as soon as I was away from the house, outside the home, on my own for a while at last, that sense of expectation consumed me, the sense of there being so much that lay ahead. So much I knew nothing about, which was going to happen.

And now. Judith, suspended. The landscape flat and without bounds. On the bridge, as she looks down into the river's rushing water, its movement does not tug at her the way it did for me when I was nine or twelve or sixteen and longing to be away. There's a point below that, which is where Judith is now. In the water, underneath it all, she lies on her back. She sees herself lying there, her eyes are open, but she doesn't know what she sees.

Judith lost Myrto, but how long is she going to stand there looking down into that river? I want her to tear herself away and move on, but it's not up to me to decide.

The girls have gone now. I didn't notice them leave. I imagine I know them, that I pack my things up and leave with them: we go down the escalator together, glide down through the huge library space, soldiers from an alien planet, arrived on Earth with our luminous pages inside the covers of our books, in the black bags over our shoulders, a whole world we've brought with us, and no one knows.

I was in Minneapolis with my publisher, the one who turned fifty, a few years ago. I knew then that I would write something that took place there. L was ill, but it was still more than a year before he died. What part of the writer knows that this or that place has a novel for me? What part of the external place connects with the internal place where writing happens? So many places, nearly all, are places we merely pass through, and never write about. And then, suddenly, something will open and reveal itself, that's what it feels like to the part of me that writes, like a way in, something that only that particular place can provide. And if I don't go there, the novel won't be found.

It's like falling in love with someone. Think of all the people we meet. And then suddenly someone's there, wide open. That person is the one, that exact person, and only them. If we don't go to them, that gleaming, beckoning thing will not be ours. I'm not sure if it's promise, but it's certainly hope. Anyway, that's what it was like with M, he was the one.

//

Writing isn't normally difficult. It's just writing. Stating what I see. But with M it's something unclear, shifting. I don't know what I'm seeing, and I can't remember either.

That's the most difficult thing about this novel. It's like the heart of it just keeps on pumping blood no matter what. It won't be still. My heart, be still so I can look at you, so I can hold you in my hand, so I can clutch you to my chest and never lose you again. But the heart will not. The heart keeps on. The heart wants to live. It doesn't care about me.

The bird flies right into us. The warm night, the circular beam picking out the sandy, rocky road that winds between the dark edges of the lava. I'm sat behind M on the scooter and all of a sudden this big bird is flapping in our faces, the scooter swerves, and the bird is lying there, as if dead. M stops and goes back, he picks up the bird in both hands and looks at me, then puts it in the luggage box. Back at the cottage we don't know what to do. M holds it up in the bright light of the outside lamp, and the only thing we hear is the sea, we're almost in Africa here. The bird is pale in colour and speckled brown, the beak is curved like a pickaxe, and when M takes it out of the box it wakes up, it lunges at him and flaps its wings. Let it go, I shriek, but M keeps hold, he laughs out loud. Let it go, I shriek again, only it won't fly. He puts it back in the box on the scooter where the rats won't get it, or the fox, whatever. The next day, when morning comes, it's gone.

I don't know if M's going to come, to the island where I've rented an old fisherman's cottage at the tip of a headland, three weeks in August, a small volcanic island south of Lampedusa. The cottage is just a single oblong room, innermost behind a curtain is the bed. I never know if M's going to come, or what it's going to be like if he does. It's the same in Milan. I just never know. But when he does come, and we're together, I feel so alive. Every moment, no matter if it hurts, no matter if it's terrible, is so intense then, it bursts open, and everything else is shoved out to the edges. To look at M, for me, is to look straight into life.

//

It's like there's an extra level of energy in him, when he puts his foot to the ground it's as if his body's already on the upstroke again, ready for more, he's strong and sinewy at the same time, my fingers reach around his wrist. He wears wire-rimmed glasses that make him look like a student, his work trousers are thin and soft, his hands are rough, the nails worn down as if he works with strong chemicals, but that's not why, it's because he bites them. He never bites his nails when he's with me. He comes to fix the cistern, the water's running out of it like a waterfall into the toilet and the stopcock won't work, it's my friend Camilla who lives in the same building that gives me his number.

It's a year since L died. I'm not ready in any way, when I go out I look at the ground. A few days later M texts me, something about the apartment, the light. Smiley and a kiss emoji. It confuses me – he's so young, what's he after? I tell myself he's just being friendly. I'm at home in Oslo. After a while, I send him a photo from the kitchen there.

He comes and picks me up at the airport when I get back. I emerge from arrivals with my suitcase and bag, he appears in front of me – work clothes, T-shirt, the dark warmth of evening. We say nothing, and don't smile either, his eyes are serious and brown. I let go of my bag and we hold each other. He's completely open, trembles, lets me hold everything that's in him. It's how he holds me too.

On our way into the city he turns off and takes us up a hill, to a park of some kind, a small wooded area, and a mist descends, a kind of night mist that wisps around the trees as we go up the hill. There's no one else there. We smoke a joint while leaning against a stone wall, there's such a softness between us, we touch each other with our eyes, stroke each other as carefully as we can.

The following weekend he takes me with him to Bergamo, in the white van with his tools in the back and sheets of paper strewn across the dashboard, we park in the shade down a side street. Will you be able to find your way back here, I ask as we walk away. He wheels round and carries on walking, backwards for a moment, smiling. I reckon so, he says.

Him in a grey T-shirt and me with bare arms in a thin silk dress, he's so boyish, his strong arms, his eyes are so kind, his nose with its little upturn, it's like he's listening with all his being, he's so loose and vulnerable, like an animal that's just woken up.

We go up the steps, pausing here and there to look over the wall at the view. After we get to the top, we walk about among all the people, the buildings in the upper town: his straight posture, his smooth skull seen from behind, the smell of detergent on his clothes when I get close, his every step draws the fabric of his trousers tight across his thighs. At one point, he whispers that men are looking at me, I can tell by his voice that it's something he likes, and it makes me feel happy. Inside the café above the cable railway he finds a table by the window, orders coffee, we gaze far into the flat landscape as the carriages glide up and down. I can't remember if he takes my hand, but inside me it's as if he's been holding it the whole time, even then.

That evening he smooths his hand gently over my shoulder, we're standing in my living room, he looks at my shoulder, then at me, then back at my shoulder again, his brown eyes, he kisses the bump of my shoulder bone, pulls my strap aside, it slips down over my arm, he kisses my arm, bends forwards and kisses my neck below my ear, then picks me up and carries me into the bedroom and puts me down gently on the bed, sits down on the edge and looks at me, smooths his fingers over my dress, looks at the hand as he smooths, looks up at me, smooths upwards from my knee to my thigh, then the other, and he's looking at me the whole time, that's it, he says softly, yes, that's it, here, and he pushes my knee out to the side, look how fine you are, he says, and he says my name, several times, he says my name, he whispers my name, and it's his hands that are saying it, and his eyes, saying, seeing, seeing my name, who I am.

He picks me up round the corner or further up the street. So no one will come through the entrance door and see us, together. He knows nearly everyone in the building, but it's his mother he's afraid of, that she should get wind of what's going on, though it's not his parents who live here, it's his aunt who does. He's seventeen years younger than me. By the time he was born, we'd moved from Finnmark to Oslo, we left the dog behind, and the landscape, the river and the plain, had already become something inside me that no one else knew about.

I look at M, his eyes are on the road, he turns the steering wheel through the bends, says nothing, the radio, music, his face sits so heavily inside me, as if he was a stone sculpture in my stomach, weighing me down. It's the middle of summer, we're at the sea, a place where his parents have a small apartment, but he'd rather go up into the woods, and I think, as he turns off onto the narrow track where black-painted holiday cottages stand in a row, slowing down almost to a halt in front of the last house to tell me it used to be theirs before they sold it and bought the apartment near the beach, that it's something he's been wanting to show me, he's been wanting to take me with him back into his childhood. So you used to play here, I say, because there's a yellow field across the way, among these low-slung hills, and I can almost see him as I gaze out, a small M passing through the meadow, and he smiles quietly as if we both can see him, and says yes.

He pulls up at a picnic spot with a decaying table and a rusty rectangular barbecue, we put the bags down on the table, meat and vegetables (red peppers, courgette), M opens a beer and tips the charcoal into the barbecue, gets it lit and burning. The dog tears down to the riverbank and back again, along the track, into the woods, back again, a sheep-dog. It was here they would go swimming when they had the house. He's brought everything we need, a chopping board, oil and salt, he spreads out the packets of meat, de-seeds the peppers and chops them into big pieces, it's so quiet in the shade of the trees by the dusty unmade track, the river has almost no water left in it, and he has a way of being in the outdoors that feels so like home, so familiar.

After we've eaten we go for a swim. I get cold after only a short while and climb back up onto the bank, but M and the dog stay in the water for some time, it's as if he's become a boy again, forgetting everything around him, wanting to investigate and see, he dives after small fish and becomes quite preoccupied in a shallow pool, turning onto his side and letting the water run over his young body. Afterwards, he falls asleep in the sun on the blue rug. I don't know where I am myself in this recollection, I see him from a distance, I suppose I was somewhere in the shade at the side of the track, sitting there waiting and looking at him, looking at him as he lay there sleeping on the rug, his whole person, in wet bathing shorts, on the white sand, so close, and at the same time so closed, so far away inside himself.

Pappa in the Dead Sea, he served in Gaza after he completed his training in nursing and pastoral care, he's floating in the water, his slender young body outstretched, and is smiling sheepishly, his hair as yet quite dark, I was still small when he started going grey at the temples, now all he has is thin wisps of white. And the ones of him in his nurse's coat, where his smile seems buried away, whereas in others he's laughing, his head tipped back, one in front of a pyramid on a trip to Egypt. The shoebox with the photographs in it, I locked the door of my room in Tana and sat down on the floor and removed the lid and took out the photos one by one, holding each up in turn and looking at it, spreading them out around me on the floor, and it was such a momentous thing for me, to sit there and look at them all, and see that the insanely handsome, pensive-looking man in those photographs was my father.

One evening we go past the first place I lived with L. There, I say, pointing, behind those windows. M says he went to secondary school in the same building, his classroom was behind the same windows. So where I sat on the sofa learning Italian with L, in the same room M once sat behind a desk and had a crush on a girl in his class. Another time, M pulls up in front of a building close by. You see the balcony on the third floor, he says, and I tip my head back, it's a narrow balcony extending across three windows. That's where we lived when I was a boy, he says, we lived there all the time I was growing up, and when we turn the corner I see that the gateway is directly across the street from the building where L kept a studio. The studio windows are dark, we stand in the light from the street lamps under the tall trees, I look through the iron gate into the courtyard where M once must have pedalled about on his trike, much later he got a motor scooter, and it's as if I can see him, returning home at night, in the dark; I try not to think of other women, I think only about him, coming home on his own, going in through the gate, letting himself in at the door, climbing the stairs, back up the stairs, to them. And now, his aunt, he visits her still, either on his own or with his parents, the fact that she lives in the same building as me.

As if we were meant to meet. As if something twined our bodies together by connecting our places, long before we had any idea. There's a reason we're together. Something has set the stage for us, prepared the way, something in time itself has insisted that sooner or later it had to be us.

//

I start waiting at two o'clock. We were meant to be travelling down together, only M got into some trouble and so we agreed that I should go on ahead. I walk with my backpack on, to a park with tall palm trees in it. I sit on various benches where there's some shade, read a book, without any idea which one, look at my phone, it's in my hand the whole time. I've come by plane, he's driving down. It was his mother, she likes to go to the market, it's right next to where they live, M caught sight of her as he was going past in the van, it was early and so he double-parked, jumped out, he wanted to surprise her, but as he approached from behind, as he weaved his way through all the marketgoers, two young men stepped in ahead of him, one of them already had hold of her handbag when M intervened with a punch to the face, and then another, they lost some teeth, those two young men, and pressed charges against him, and the day we're meant to be going is the day he has to appear in court. At six o'clock the light softens, at seven it's dark, at eight the park closes. I sit for a while on a low wall. He texts me the name of the hotel. I start walking, following the dots on Google Maps, along a very busy road by the harbour, the lights from the cars in the dark, their strong yellows, their reds and blues.

And then he's there, suddenly he's there in the car, right alongside me, his face in the darkness behind the window, and the world begins to turn again, like a merry-go-round.

He's booked a room for us overlooking the big square and the old theatre with its faded colours, we're going to be on holiday together for a week. Everything's new. The first morning, we drive to a beach just outside the city, the area's packed, we can't park anywhere, we drive around in the vicinity, eventually there's a spot where M's certain we'll get a fine, I suggest we carry on a bit further, we can always walk back, but M parks anyway. The sun and the dust as we go back to the beach. We hire a parasol on the *Beach for Police Officers and their Families*, and laugh about it. Smoking's not even allowed. We lie on our sunbeds in the shade, M swims for some time, I drink a beer. It's his eyes, I can't say what it is that I see in them, I become unsure of the warmth that's there so strongly in them sometimes, but then becomes hard and excluding, I don't know what that warmth means, if it's something I can trust, if it's going to hold, if it's still there, in behind, even when it can't be seen.

The next day we drive inland, M wants to look in on a fireman friend of his, he buys a big boxful of cream biscuits and carries it with both hands as we go towards the door of the break room or the duty room or whatever it is, and the firemen get to their feet from their chairs and the sofa and come up to the worktop in the kitchen area where the biscuits are lifted out of their wrapping, and it's all people and voices, and the coffee maker.

Afterwards we go outside, his friend is older, they're in a motorcycle club together, most of the members are firemen or in the military or the police, they've ridden through the desert several times, in Tunisia. They smoke and chat about people they know and things I know nothing about, I lie down on a bench in the shade and close my eyes and think I might as well have a rest while they're talking.

Another motorcycle friend lives out on the plain, we drive through a built-up area where white industrial sheds line the road, looking for the right number, and eventually we pull up outside a tall fence, and behind it there's a single-storey house with a flat roof, and a shed in there too. M presses the buzzer, we wait, he presses again, and after a minute someone inside responds, and we sit there in the car as the big gate opens in front of us, clatters and scrapes as it's drawn aside.

M's friend is well over seventy, his wife looks younger, there's some family there too, around a swimming pool, they come into view when we go round to the other side, daughters and their husbands, grandchildren, a baby wrapped in white, held against a shoulder. We're offered water, I'd have liked a beer or a glass of wine, M sits down with his friend, what about me, the man's wife seems nice enough, a bit sad perhaps, and all the others going in and out of the house, I say I need to take a call and go with my phone in my hand, my earbuds, to the place at the front where we parked, there's a tall hedge at the far end, and in its narrow strip of shade, for as long as I can, I hold an earbud to my ear as I pace slowly backwards and forwards.

And all the time, I long for the softness in his eyes. The part of him that's naked. To be with him there. Where nothing is in doubt.

His friend is this big-deal wholesaler of some sort, he's booked us into a hotel close by, we drive there and shower before we're due to meet up with them again and go on somewhere else, to a small town by the sea where M's friend has invited us out to a restaurant. His wife's in a full-length dress, gold jewellery, plenty of make-up, and one of the grandchildren's coming with us too, a five-year-old girl who sits between M and me on the back seat, she's playing on her tablet device, it makes all sorts of noises and keeps flashing, blue and green and yellow, and that's what I remember from driving to the restaurant, that we look at each other over the top of this little girl's head with all these noises going off and different coloured lights flashing.

Big plates of seafood are brought to the table, it all seems to land in front of M's friend and it's as if he devours everything at an astonishing rate while the rest of us sit watching, even if that's not really what happens. The little girl sits with her device at the end of the table and at one point it makes such a racket that M's friend explodes and yells at her, everyone's quiet after that, and he turns round again and starts talking to someone at another table.

There's an empty fountain on the square in front of the hotel, we don't get back until late, the place is dark, but the owner has shown us how to get in after they've gone to bed. We go over to the fountain and M rolls a joint, takes a few drags and offers it to me, I smoke some too, and we go towards the entrance, we're driving on the next day, just the two of us. In the reception area I suddenly feel dizzy, it must be the joint, I sink down into the nearest chair, buildings angle and vault towards me, faces dissolve into mine, and by the time I'm okay again it feels like I've been gone for hours. Not even a minute, says M, and helps me to the room.

The next morning we find a café, a white table in a street, under a white parasol. It's three months since we first met, his ex is still living in their apartment, he says it's over and that she's moving out, but she's still there, he says he sleeps downstairs on the sofa, because if he goes upstairs, they'll end up having sex.

I ask what he's looking for. What do you want with me, what's the idea, this holiday? M starts crying. He says he doesn't know. I take it to mean he's not really looking for anything. That he's not that bothered about me, at least not enough for it to be worth my while sticking around. I say that to him. He's drunk his coffee, doesn't want anything to eat, but fidgets with his serviette, folding it, twisting it, clutching it while his tears drip onto the table.

I get to my feet and go along the street a bit, check the train times on my phone, then go back and tell him I'm taking the first one that leaves. He gets up, and we go back to the car. But first we've got to stop off at another café, all gilded edges and waiters in uniform, M's friend has texted and said he's there with his wife, their plates show the remains of some cream buns, we have a quick coffee and thank him for dinner and the room. I find the station on my phone, it's close by. M swings up in front of a white building, the platform's right behind it, the station itself is closed, but there's a sign saying the trains are still stopping. M wants to wait with me. We both stand crying in the heat, in the shade of the white building, me just a bit, M the whole time, sobbing, as if he's wringing himself out, wringing his tears from his stomach. I find it strange that he can cry so much, he's the one dragging his feet, not me.

The train comes, a dusty local train with only one coach, we hug and his body thumps against mine, pounding and trembling, I get on and he just stands there on the platform, his eyes are red, his whole face is wet, as the doors close he hands me something before wheeling round and running back to where the car is on the other side of the station building. The train pulls away. I look down, it's the serviette he was fidgeting with at the café, it must have been in his pocket. It's not a serviette any more, he's folded and twisted it into a stem with a single leaf and a head, what I'm holding in my hand is a rose.

//

Innermost, below the window, was the bed. My room, the long narrow maid's room, behind the kitchen. I must have lain down to sleep there every night from when I was sixteen until I was eighteen, we lived there when we moved to Oslo again, the whole family, Pappa and my brothers, all of us. It had been Mamma's long-term plan, to wait, to stick it out, year after year, until it was time for us to start upper secondary, so that she could use that as her lever, or else we'd have to get student rooms in Vadsø. Why couldn't she just have taken us with her and gone? She was in charge of the social services department in Nesseby, had been part of the committee that had drawn up the new social services law, why couldn't she have applied that law to herself?

We started at different schools, all three of us. My younger brother still had a couple of years left of lower secondary. Majorstuen School. Their rooms were next to each other, the room where my younger brother slept was separated from our parents' room by a partition wall. I was the only one so far away, out there on a limb, a twig.

My left knee hurts as I'm writing this. My left knee hurts because I tore my meniscus when I was seventeen and living there. I hadn't realised until now, as I'm writing, how things are connected. The washing machine was just outside my room, in the kitchen. Some nights it'd be running a cycle. Those were nights when I didn't need to listen, because I wouldn't have heard anything anyway. I couldn't watch out then. They were nights when I could lie down in that bed and sleep.

//

He texts me, a couple of weeks have gone by, he asks me how I am. If we can meet. Of course we can. From out of the darkness on the other side of the canal he comes towards me, squeezes my hand, there's a strip of grass alongside the wall, he's got the dog with him. We sit down, legs dangling above the water, talk softly, mostly we're just quiet. Looking, seeing.

And then, days when I hardly hear from him. But then he'll be there again, I wait for him upstairs, a glass of prosecco in my hand, he comes dancing towards me from the lift and in through the open door.

I invite him to Oslo. I'm touring a performance with a singer and a guitarist, but if he comes to the last night maybe he could stay a few days? I'm not at all sure he'll come, but when eventually we're about to begin I see him sitting there, at a table at the side. He's come all the way there from Gardermoen, by train and ferry and bus, walked the last part of the way up the gravel road to Hellviktangen, even though he's never been to Norway before, never been to Denmark or to London or to Paris either, and his English isn't very good, but there he is, sitting by one of the steamed-up PVC windows in the packed marquee, and when we come in and take the stage, he looks at me, he has to twist his body to look at me, and it's as if he lifts from his chair, as if he's directing himself towards me, over the heads of all the other people seated there, and in his eyes there's no more resistance, no reservation, only a warmth as powerful as my father's torch shining at me across the heather.

The days that follow – he's so quiet. You're so quiet, I say, and he musters a smile, as if he's pleased and ever so slightly proud that I've asked, about him, the person he is, doesn't he know I'm always interested in the person he is, only now I'm asking in order to draw him out towards me, towards us. You don't know me yet, he says, the person I am, my *caratteraccio*, and he looks at me. His bad temper, okay, but I'm not really listening, and imagine anyway that his softness will come out stronger, it's the softness that's most important, truest, it's what we are, we're the nakedness at our core, fragile.

On a bench at the Paradisbukta bathing spot, Oslo Fjord stretched out in front of us, salmon wraps and a Thermos of coffee, he's not saying anything, his face isn't showing me anything, I don't know, I'm walking behind Pappa on the fell, the dog's run on ahead somewhere, my brothers are either side of me, and behind Pappa's big blue rucksack I walk, fishing rod in hand, Pappa in his flared jeans and trainers, his legs so strong in the heather, all I do is see, this is Pappa, and when he turns round, because all of a sudden he will, stop and turn round, I'm waiting for it, it's the look in his eyes then, angry or not, if he smiles it'll feel like I'm exploding with joy. So handsome he is, M, so handsome it hurts. He looks out over the water. Doesn't it matter that to come here he got vaccinated, which he's against, that he actually came? Of course it does. But I want more. I need more. I need to be all the way inside where the warmth is. If he's keeping me away from there, then being together doesn't mean a thing.

I bring a bottle of champagne along every time we go out to see the city, I've still got so much left over from the wedding two years ago, L was so ill, we hardly drank any of it. So we drink champagne on the beach at Bygdøy, champagne at Akershus Fortress, with the harbour and the city hall and Aker Brygge in front of us, it's cold but nice anyway, and we can always pop into Kiwi and buy a couple of beers if we run out of champagne, and in the evenings we drink wine. On the last night of his visit, after Bygdøy and a strong afternoon cocktail at a friend's, I want us to linger at the top of the hill, St. Hanshaugen, on our way home, I've still got a couple of beers in my bag, I open mine and hand the other to M, but he doesn't want one, he just stares into the air in front of him. All night in bed, he pushes me away.

The next morning I get up on my own, first, I try my best to be quiet. An hour later, M appears, doesn't look at me, yanks a chair out from under the table. He doesn't want any bread, shoves his coffee cup away. Never a night! It comes so abruptly, Pappa banging a fist on the table. He says a drink now and again is okay, but this is getting too much. Never a night without! He jumps to his feet, his voice is hard, he says it again, several times, his words stream in the air, it's the drinking, but at the same time it's more than that, something inside him, twisting and growing, a dense, red cloud, he says so again, and again after that, Yes, I say. Can't he stop? Yes. I see what he means, but I don't know how to deal with it otherwise, my unease. It hurts so much. He's completely closed. It's not going to change. He's right. I've ruined things, it's me who's done it. I can't remember what we do next, and then he leaves.

Back in Milan, M's bought the best seats, the whole courtyard's filled with candles, they're all over the ground, on pedestals, on ledges, everywhere. We're seated at the very front, he sits down on his chair and leans into me, his smooth skull, his coarse woollen sweater, I put my arm around him and he stays there. Among all the candles on the stage is a black piano, a women in a full-length dress enters through a door, we applaud. For the next hour she performs music from popular Italian films, I've never heard any of it before, she trills the notes and makes sweeping flourishes that are quite unbearable, but I look at the candles, they're above us too, on the balustrade, it's like an enchanted palace and we're at the ball, all I can do is look at the candles and hold, hold my arm around M.

Afterwards we go out into the darkness, into the warm streets, everyone milling out into the ordinary night, M at my side, he seems so happy, says something about it being a shame more people don't know about these concerts, the chance of listening to music in such surroundings, we step past some other people, a man says, She hit the odd duff note, and I think to myself that I hadn't noticed. When we lived in Finnmark a piano teacher would come to our house once a week and give us lessons, the three of us, for five years we took lessons, but I was never any good. I think about the candles again, M, his freshly shaved skull, we turn a corner and are on our own, in the narrow street, tall walls on both sides, the darkness is so soft. She was very good, says M, glances at me and takes my hand, strokes my hand with his thumb, even if she did hit a duff note now and again. I say nothing, squeeze his hand, look at him and smile, he's so happy, seems so proud and fulfilled, he's taken me out and given me something exceptional is what I imagine him thinking, something no one else has done for me before, but what he doesn't know, I think to myself, is that this, his hand in mine, this very moment, his feet walking next to mine, the two of us here together, passing along this street, which is here always, that all this, for me, is in every second exploding with the exceptional.

One evening in the darkness, in the park between the tall trees, M lets the dog off the lead, she runs off and comes back as we watch. I can't remember what we talk about, the important thing is not what we say but his voice, our voices together, soft and quiet, touching each other somewhere deep inside, as if with the feather emoji he sometimes puts in his texts. It's late, he's hungry, there's a food truck by the road with some folding chairs and tables outside, he orders a panini with horsemeat, a beer, while I order a bottle of water, I've already eaten, and at last I can show him I don't drink all the time.

We sit in the warm night air watching the dog run around on the grass in the park. Seventeen years older. I think about it all the time. My wrinkles, my saggy bum. Does he really want me, is it true? I asked myself the same question all the time with L, never quite believing, but with M, his age, it's like it's become even more important. In the darkness in the park he's so very much there, in this moment he's mine only, and we drift and float and flow in the softest of softness. But apart from that? All the days, the weekends, all the evenings and nights when all I want is to be with M and have no idea where he is or what he's doing, only that he's not texting me, not calling me, not coming to be with me. He's not there by my side. Doesn't that mean he doesn't want to be?

We talk about going up to Finnmark together. Midnight sun, North Cape and the northern lights, M says. I picture the road bending up to the housing estate, walking up the hill there after school, all the way to the turning space at the end of the road, where our house was.

He comes with me to Copenhagen. I'm appearing at a festival, Saturday morning in a big theatre space, M's presence pulsates at me from where he's sitting at the front, and I've no idea what I'm saying on the stage in the company of a fellow writer and friend, I've known her more than twenty years, because M and the two of us are all there is, M and what's between us, which trembles inside me, all I want is to get things over with so I can be on my own with him again, just the two of us. Afterwards we're in the green room, M's beside me, there's a critic there too, someone else I've known for years and we've exchanged books, she looks at us and there's something in her gaze, disbelief or puzzlement, or is she afraid, it seems almost like she is. How old they've become. Such predictable conversations, endless repetitions of things we've said and done and thought at least a thousand times before, the same old game. I look at M, we get to our feet, I take two beers from the fridge to drink on the train into the city on our way to Christiania, I say my thanks, see you next time, and then we leave, we go down the stairs and out through the doors. At last. I look at M, we're so happy. At last, something streaming in me that I'm not controlling, I don't know what it is, I just know that being with M is the most vital of all things to me and I want only to be immersed in it.

Others don't see it. They don't see his warmth, they don't get the person he is, the tenderness, all that glimmers and glows so deep inside. Our world, our whole universe. He shows it only to me.

We sit out on the little plastic stools on the balcony in Milan, leaning back against the wall. M smokes, it's dark, the only light is from the street down below. He tells me quietly about when he was a child, his mother left his violent father, his biological father, not the one he grew up with. I see little M in his words, M, who has to stay behind up in the mountains from when he's one until he's three, his mother having left him with a childless couple, an older couple, she went away and came back and then went away again. I ask him what it was like, it was good, he says, but how can he know, I ask myself.

Afterwards we make love on the sofa. Completely naked we're together, newborns, blind we are, and frightened and small.

11

The fog makes everything so still. In front of us is a high wire-mesh fence and a run-down building with dark windows and shutters hanging from their hinges, tall trees all around, a density of slender trunks. On the other side of the fence is where the woods begin. We stand behind the van, It's old and battered, he says, and then when he unlocks the rear doors and opens them out to the sides, I see it, the yellow light goes on in the back and illuminates his face too, we stand and look at the bike, both of us do, it's secured by some straps and his own mountain bike is in there too, he climbs inside and starts unfastening. It's a black ladies' bike from the sixties, all the original details intact. He found it in a customer's outhouse and persuaded them to sell. I've always wanted a bike like this. I tell him so. I see the way he holds back his smile, how happy it makes him. I know he's been spending time in the garage in the basement out by the other canal across town, where the city begins to peter out and there are swathes of green and trees, he's been spending time down there doing it up, inner tubes and brakes, the thin wires, the spokes gleam, the chain guard too, and when he lifts it out and puts it down gently on the ground, he shows me the dynamo, the same as I had on my very first bike, to be tucked in against the front wheel, and then, after that, we can see, as we cycle along in the fog in the fading light, on the gravel paths that follow the water in the deep trench below, then over the yellow leaves in the empty woods, the shifting beam of light that lights our way, the lamp that still works.

M veers off onto a narrower path to the left, I follow, and then he pulls up and lays his bike down on the ground, I do so too with mine. We go through a few metres of thicket and come out by a pond. We can't see far in front of us, the fog is so thick. The pond has a silvery film to it, broken by big glistening flecks, the odd toppled tree with its branches sticking up, some old plastic that's attached itself, bits of things floating, motionless. It's like we've gone behind a curtain and discovered a hidden place, the pond at the centre of everything, a place where there's no through-wind any more, where everything that isn't carried along on the whirling currents instead loses momentum and is deposited at the side and then just lies there, hesitantly almost, until enough detritus has collected and something else takes over and sort of shoves it into motion, gets it going again, a little bit more, come on, only then, eventually, when it's no longer possible to get any further, when there's nothing else left to come and carry it along, it all just collects at the side again, in the stagnant water. M reaches for my hand and gives it a squeeze, then lights a smoke. We stand there beside each other, I lean my head against his shoulder, the green army jacket's coarse fabric.

It gets dark as we cycle back. We buy two beers from a nearby bar, walk back and get in the van, M opens the bottles with his lighter. He rolls a joint and we sit there smoking and drinking beer and staring out. The trees are losing their leaves so everything's more open, light comes from a street lamp next to where we've parked, it pools and creates a space between the trees and we sit there staring into that space and it feels like a promise almost, a hope of some sort, the leaves that are closest, on which the light falls, are transparent and near-white.

//

The white feet there on the painted brown floorboards. Judith stands in her nightdress, upstairs at the sewing table. It's Sunday morning. It goes on for some weeks. The whole winter.

//

I stand in the doorway, his ex has finally moved out. Directly in front of me black shelving divides the room, there's an aquarium, the dog's dinner bowl. The floorboards are dark wood, the walls look like they used to be white, or are they just grey. The shelves are mainly empty, he's told me he's been clearing out, he's been at it for a while and didn't want me to come until he was finished. I wonder how much has gone, what it was like before. Who is he? Some carrier bags, a metal lamp, no books, but I knew that already. Behind the shelves, a black leather sofa with a solid wooden coffee table in front of it, an ashtray, a fleece blanket with a yellow pattern, above the sofa more shelves, they too empty. After the stairs, a big TV on a unit, the windows fronting onto the balcony have heavy curtains, drawn. In the corner on the right is the kitchen, with plastic strip lights under the cupboards, red heart magnets on the fridge door, on the cupboard doors too there are hearts, round red hearts he's stuck on. M looks at me. Do you like it?

Can I open the door? We step outside. The balcony faces onto the back, there are some trees, and further away, beyond the road, is the canal. His electric scooter is parked there, on the balcony, where stuff is piled up in both corners, a green bath mat and black bin bags, some bamboo sticks, nowhere to sit, it seems like he never spends time there, never uses it.

The bed is under the sloping ceiling, I think of the woman who slept in it, younger than him, from Romania, M's told me she slept the whole time, and at the back there's a small bathroom. A skylight. The upstairs has just been painted, all white, and there's a different style about it, as if the occupant was a mature woman: a grey rococo-style chair with patterned upholstery, an empty writing desk with curved legs set back against the wall. At the other end, sets of drawers and a wardrobe, racks of clothes, it's his mother who buys his clothes, there's always something new for him to wear and her taste suits him, simple lines and subdued colours, greens and greys, blues and blacks, and shirts I know she irons.

We sit for a while on the sofa. He shows me a lump of wood, a twisted root he found on a beach in the south of the country, one day he was going to make something out of it, a lampstand maybe. To put here, he says, and places a hand on the table in front of us. I hold the object for a moment, my fingertips trace its convoluted lines, I see M, he's standing on an empty beach somewhere far away. I nod.

He never misses a thing. When we go round town he'll say, Look, that guy there's got something (drugs, he means, stolen goods, dirty money, criminal stuff), any minute now he's going to take off, do a runner. And the next minute the guy actually does start running, and as if from above, like a wide-screen image, we see two other men set off after him from different directions. And what seemed like a quiet, peaceful scene just a moment before, people milling about that I'd barely even noticed, is suddenly torn open and danger spills out everywhere, here too, it's right beneath the surface, everywhere. One Sunday at the Duomo a woman is about to faint, I don't notice, her husband walking beside her doesn't notice, but M sees what's happening, they're almost behind us, but still he senses it and leaps to her aid, he grabs the woman's arm and wraps his own arm around her to stop her falling.

L's studio is still intact, the days have simply gone by, everything's the way it was that last day. It's got windows under the ceiling on three sides, so even though it's halfway below ground level, the light still floods in, and L installed track lighting too. Canvases stand stacked against the walls, in the middle of the floor there's his turquoise wing armchair, flecks of paint, in the corner two pallets of Leca blocks, he built shelves out of them, or used them for an easel with impregnated yellow wooden boards on top. I haven't known what to do about the place, it's so big, so empty. Through someone M knows, an estate agent, there's suddenly someone who wants to rent it and use it as a storeroom. It's dark when we carry the canvases down into the storage space, and they help me, M and one of his men, and there's a dismantled IVAR unit too, with all the shelves, we lug it all down the concrete stairs, the light's at the far end, and then we go back up again, we work as if in a frenzy, and they help me get rid of the felt floor covering, the brushes, we bin the shoes that have been left behind, a pair of flip-flops and the old clothes I've folded up and placed in a pile next to the armchair, the ones L wore when he was here painting, we carry the whole lot out to the containers in the back yard and bin it.

The next night M comes on his own, it's raining, and together we shift the Leca blocks on a steel dolly and load them into the van. It's late, M's been renovating a bathroom all day and has come straight from work, he doesn't look at me, his movements are hostile, they shut me out, but at least he's here, now, to help. We stack them in the back, there's just enough room. He puts his foot down to get us out of the yard, it's just a small incline, but the cobbles are slippery with rain and the heavy Leca holds us back, the wheels start spinning, there's no traction, and the van slides, he can't stop it, not until we're a hand's breadth from the wall. He manoeuvres it away so we can open the back doors and unload some of the blocks. Our faces are drenched, we stack the blocks on the ground, M works twice as quickly as me. Eventually he's able to get the van up the incline, he stops the engine, pulls the handbrake on, and then we have to lug the Leca blocks from where we left them, in the rain, and load them back into the van. He's in a bad mood, but I'm grateful nevertheless, I'd never have been able to do it on my own. When we're finished, he gets in, the window's open, the rain pouring down, his glasses, his wet face. Are you going to eat, something like that is what I must have asked him, just for something to say, I suppose, a new possibility of sorts, but he tightens his jaw, dinner's a long way off yet, he says, he's got to go to the garage first, all the way out there, and unload all *this*, the backwards nod of his head, my Leca blocks, my fault, I realise that, of course I do, but I understand him as well, he must be exhausted, all day he's been working and when finally evening comes round he has to come here and do all this, he offered to himself, only then there was all that rain, the overloaded van, and everything got so frantic and took so much longer than we'd thought.

The open window in the rain, M's eyes, I see more in them now than in the beginning, now it's as if those eyes have seen all the world's pain, every kind of sorrow, as if they feel everything that hurts, no denigration left unknown to them, and at the same time they can be so warm, so full of goodness, so gentle. I remember many years ago when I was younger than M is now and married to the father of my daughter, it was dark then too, and late in the evening, I came home, I'd been away a night or two at some writers' thing or other, I came up the hill to the townhouse where we lived and I saw him standing there on the balcony leaning back against the wall smoking. The look he gave me then from the kitchen balcony, his eyes directing down at me there on the road, there was such warmth in that look. It made me angry. I shut him out. It was as if his warmth hurt, as if it was a demand, and I couldn't deal with it, I came in through the door and was angry, when all he wanted was to welcome me home with kindness. Is that what it's like for M? That the will is there, only sometimes he can't? He drives out through the gateway, the van lurches as he wrenches the wheel to turn onto the road. He doesn't look back, doesn't wave goodbye. Behind the wheel he looks strong and small at the same time. I stand there until he's gone, not knowing when I'll see him next, how many days it'll take before it's all blown over, before he's in a different place, in a good mood again.

I'm walking home in the rain in Milan, only it's Tana when Pappa was building the house, the early eighties, a dark hole in the ground where the road bends, and Pappa and my brother are standing in it, my eldest brother, the one who went to England and stayed there, he was twelve, he had to help, every evening after dinner he'd have to go with Pappa up to the dark hole in the ground, mud and grime everywhere, it must have been cold, two floodlights angled to where they were working. The two of them laying the foundation, polystyrene blocks all the way round, then pouring the cement inside that hardened like bricks, and Pappa was always in a mood when they were working, fuming, the whole time, I felt so sorry for my brother, my younger brother was too little and I was excused because I was a girl, Pappa said, I didn't think it was much of an excuse, no one did, but we said nothing, it was a relief and it was a weight, and then the wall that was inside Pappa when they came home, his arms and his broad chest in his red checked shirt, never a good word about my brother, that he was a hard worker and never shy to get stuck in, not a word, and I made waffles, cinnamon buns, raisin buns, *hvetekrans* and *rullekake*, so there'd be something nice for them when they got in, I did it for my brother's sake, and for my own, it was a way of playing a part, even if it didn't count, because I knew I was excused from the worst of all, which was Pappa, excused from being where he was, evening after evening, and not being able to say anything, not being able to go home, having to stand there, my brother, in the floodlighting.

But there was light in Pappa too. Light in his eyes, it was Pappa who would turn towards me in the kitchen one morning when the house was finished, upstairs in the kitchen with its splendid view across the valley, he stood with his back to me frying bacon and eggs, and then turned as I came into the kitchen, and there was the wallpaper we'd chosen, he and I together, in Vadsø, we'd stood and turned the pages of those big wallpaper books together and I'd sat next to him as we drove through the bends, the road following the line of the fjord, and it wasn't Mamma who was sitting there next to him and was going to choose, it was me, and again it was a weight and it was a gift, and then, that morning, in the kitchen, he turned and looked at me and his eyes were alight and something in him was wide open, it was a kind of joy, and he said, Do you know what I dreamed about, and I just looked at him and smiled and he smiled back at me and there was that great open landscape in his eyes, the high fells above Ørsta where he grew up and would lead the sheep in summer when he was a little boy, and there was China too, and the blue barn door on which they carried my grandmother across the river when he was born, my father, a Chinese prince. A bird, Pappa said, an enormous bird, there was this enormous bird that came, with a huge wingspan, and I picture the bird flying through the air above Pappa's head, so beautiful it is, majestic and wild, and it settled here, he says, and pats his left shoulder, here it sat, and its beak was a rainbow beak, he says, a beak in all sorts of colours, and I picture the beak too, and then it told me something, he says, What did it say, I ask him, it must have been something gleaming, something glittering, something big and wonderful, the message the bird had to deliver like that, into Pappa's ear, and Pappa fixes me for a moment, and that's when it changes, the look in his eyes, a shadow comes over them, a line at an angle, and it's the bird that's casting the shadow, that's flapping its wings, and Pappa looks at me, he looks at me the whole time, and then he says, What it said? and it hurts to look at that shadow, I want to wipe it away, to swipe the bird away, and Pappa is still looking at me, there's the smell of bacon, there's the rising, falling rumble of the cement mixer, the cement in the dented old cement mixer, Well, Pappa says and looks out of the window then, a low, violet ribbon of light in the distance, you see, he says, and turns towards the bacon again, he breaks an egg, it sizzles in the pan, breaks another, what the bird said, Pappa says, is a secret.

//

We cast Tana ahead of us, a promise, a golden ribbon. It's in our eyes when we look at each other, in what we say when we say other things, the trip becomes a part of our days, and it's no longer the housing estate I think about, but the first place, the mouth of the river, where we lived when Mamma left.

We sit by the wall in the Chinese restaurant where we're always the only non-Chinese, because it doesn't look like a restaurant from the street, more like storage, you have to edge your way in past stacks of cardboard boxes and the refrigerated display that's stuffed with we're not sure what, chicken feet and tendons and flattened-out pig's ears, and then you go round a partition into the little eating area with tables and white tablecloths and glaring strip lights. He phoned just after lunch and asked if I was doing anything tonight, if I fancied coming here with him for something to eat, he came and picked me up behind my building shortly after nine. I've already put it to the back of my mind what he was like on the way here, I put everything to the back of my mind if it doesn't feel right, he's been quiet the whole time, angry in a way, I don't know, don't know if it's us or something else, he's just quiet and closed, it helps a bit when we place our order, we're together then in choosing what we want, and we like trying new things that we wouldn't normally eat, like seaweed and kidneys and tendons, which is what we order, and the food comes and our attention's on the food while we eat, on eating the food with chopsticks, we don't need to say anything much then, it's as if we come together in eating, though he doesn't smile. There's a bigger room along a passage further inside, we can hear the sound of voices, Chinese, but we've never eaten in there. Now we've finished. M still has some warm sake in a cup, in a few minutes we'll get up and go. But hang on, does it have to be like that? Why go out for dinner if we're not going to make a nice time of it, if there's no fun, no closeness between us, no tenderness, no laughs, no everyday exuberance, if I can't feel the way I'm dying to feel as I sit across the table from him, I've looked forward all day to seeing him. My boy. And it's coming from that place that I ask, from the softness inside me, from the warmth that wants only to touch him: What do you want with me, exactly? And immediately his face hardens. Christ, and he slaps his napkin down on the table. Can't we just have a nice, quiet night out, without you probing? The front of my body stiffens, everything that's facing him becomes smooth and shiny. What I was feeling has gone. All I do is look at him, see him, the hardness in his eyes, his cheekbones, his rough hands, I see the table and the brown soy sauce and the dark green threads of seaweed that remain on the plate, the red cayenne pepper corns, I see it all, but I feel nothing. I didn't mean it like that. My first thought is that he's overreacting, to be so angry about so little. We get up and go out into the darkness, find the van, get in. I'm thinking about my question the whole time. He glances over his shoulder, pulls out. It wasn't so slight a question after all. What he wants with me, it's basically questioning our whole relationship, it was stupid of me to put it like that. I tell him so. I tell him I'm sorry. But now he's seething. All the way home through the empty streets, round the corner to the back of my building, where he lets me out.

The next day he phones me around eleven while I'm at the gym, his bright voice in the van on his way from one job to another, he makes some silly noises, I thought he was angry only he's not, I laugh, and he's even sillier then, I laugh and laugh, and there, he says, I made you laugh today as well, and I can hear that he's smiling, we hang up, and there's a blue sky, sunshine zigzagging between the buildings, all the way onto the treadmill where I'm walking and walking with my earphones in, up the steep slope.

He doesn't say show me your books. Even though they're all on the shelf in the bedroom, the bottom shelf, like in Oslo. He never says I'm proud of you when I get translated into a new language or send him a video from the reception in my honour high up among the skyscrapers in New York. He has the three that have been translated into Italian, the two that are novels he's only skimmed, the one I wrote when L was ill he's read twice, as if it's something he can apply, something that's real life. He lets me see his storerooms, the ones in the garage, he rolls up the doors of each in turn and it's like peering into a secret place, a hidden world, this is where he is when evening comes, shelves of all sorts of tools, sorted into categories, and the three motorbikes, strong and gleaming, like wild animals they stand there, one bigger than the next, which he rides in the woods and the hills, when he's on his own, with time to himself. Or in the desert, he says, that's where he uses the smallest of them, the lightest one, so it won't sink. One Sunday we go out to the woods to find mushrooms. I make us some lunch to take with us, bread rolls with tuna and egg, it starts raining as we make a path up the slope, through the trees. There's no one else around. All day we spend in the wet, misty woods, we sit in the heather on a pair of carrier bags, with a Thermos of tea, me under the hood of my anorak, M with his head bare, and the rain runs down over his scalp, his glasses. His soft nose, his freckles, his lips. We're quiet. Sometimes we look at each other and smile. I think often that it's the most precious of all the things we have together, this quietness. We don't find any mushrooms. But on the way back there's a van parked in a lay-by with boxes of them, M buys a bagful, enough for our dinner, the rest to take back home with him to his parents.

The idea comes to me of celebrating my birthday, my first party after L died. A girlfriend of mine, an art curator, offers to make risotto. M comes in the afternoon with a big yellow bag full of stuff, a ham slicer, biscuits his mother baked, confectioneries, jars of preserved fruit to go with the cheese. He's so light, so buoyant, and while I'm getting things ready in the living room he stays in the kitchen in his dark suit with my friend, I hear their voices, they're talking about food.

When everyone's arrived I get up and present them all, say a few words about each in turn, there are people from the book world, a translator, a philosopher, Camilla and her husband who's a musician, there's my friend who's done the risotto, a designer, an architect and a well-known photographer, and about M I say that he's my boyfriend, that he runs his own business and has an Australian sheepdog, I say something about all the things he can do and everything he does, so much love.

I stand with my drink over by the food all evening, at one point M's talking to some others at the opposite end of the room, he gesticulates, the flap of his jacket dances, they're talking politics. Later we carry the cake into the living room, I blow out the candles, someone takes some photos and in the photos you can see we're together, M in his suit and me beside him in my pink sequined dress, behind us L's Wegner chairs at the table.

Afterwards, the feeling of having tricked everyone. Tricked them into coming to my party. The woman in the dress in the photos. Who is she exactly? The feeling of there being such a long way to everyone else. Someone wants me to sit down with them on the sofa, but I'm too on edge to sit down. I prefer to stand. I can't remember talking to anyone.

I must have done, obviously. As if everything was all too much. At the same time, I was so glad to have them there. Too glad, perhaps. Or too sad. I don't know. As if it was all about something other than what was going on, which was being in the living room with music and wine and chatting and eating. What, then? I stood there at the table, it was more than enough to watch everything from a distance, like it was the only way I could cope with being there.

How can I believe anyone wants to be with me, if I'm not there myself? If I'm not actually anywhere. Where is the part of me that is me? The room, filled with these people who're my friends, and M sitting there at the other end. I watch him, I see him talk, but I can't remember him looking at me that evening, looking at me across the room, not once that he stops and turns, his eyes on me, to embrace me, to say we're together, the two of us.

//

I wake up around two in the night and he's not there in bed with me, he must still be downstairs, and I'm afraid, I don't know why. I go down and he's sitting leaning forwards on the sofa with his elbows on his knees, with his phone, and he doesn't look up at me. I stand still on the bottom stair, Aren't you coming to bed, I ask quietly. And straight away that hard look. Is it possible? As if I said something totally unreasonable. But he's angry, bang, just like that. Is it actually possible? He shakes his head. Can't you just leave me here in peace.

I think there's no point in me being there, in that situation. I vaguely remember I've been waiting for an opportunity, something I can act on. Because there's something between us that isn't good, even if I haven't been able to put my finger on it, but then, at that moment, it's as if I've reached the limit, something becomes clear to me, and I start packing my bag with M right there on the sofa, even angrier now, he can barely contain himself, he keeps saying the same thing over and over again, that surely it's possible for him to just sit there on his own after a long day, and of course that wasn't what I meant, I was just wondering where he was, but he's not listening, and it's like he doesn't see me either, as if he's in a trance of some kind, and his words just banging away like he was already angry before I came down the stairs. This isn't working, he says, us two, is that what he's been sitting here thinking about, is that why he's angry, we're just not compatible, he says, and then I say something like *You don't have to see me again*, but also, when I'm ready and about to leave, *Aren't you going to hold me*, only he won't, he won't even get up, and all I can do then is put my bike helmet on and go out the door, and maybe I'm not happy, but I'm at least relieved, and yes, I feel free as I cycle home, almost fly home, through Milan's empty streets.

I'm going to Oslo the next day, but there are some things M had with him for the party and since his aunt lives in the same building I just put them back in his yellow bag and leave them outside her door. She knows M was at my birthday, he told me, with pride, told me that he'd told her, and I find it odd, am I supposed to feel honoured that he mentioned me to his family. Still, it's the practical solution, and I leave a note, too, that says *For M.* I put my copy of *Mio, My Son* in there as well, and write in it, *To my M*, I write, with the date and my name underneath, and what did I do that for, it was L who published it in Italian.

I leave the bag there after the gym and sometime in the afternoon the aunt must have found it there outside her door because then M starts sending me texts, one after another, furious, and calling me too, and I just let it ring,

I can't be bothered, *Have you no guts to answer me?* he texts, and eventually I pick it up and he shouts at me for a whole hour, the same as the night before, over and over again, the same thing, his hard, incantational voice: NEVER mention his aunt's, his mother's or father's name, YOU ARE NEVER to go anywhere near MY FAMILY.

Then I go to Oslo and am just relieved to be so far away. Like he's now been cut off, I feel neither sadness nor loss. Not warmth and not longing either, no softness, no hurt. No nothing. It's not me telling me so, it's the way it actually is, as if the body has turned its back on him, something in me saying: Stop. Finished. No more.

I tell everyone I meet. About the yellow bag and ANYWHERE NEAR my family. I'm having dinner with a fellow writer, there are several of us from the publishing house, my publisher's there too, and I'm outraged and, well, afraid? Everyone listens and nods earnestly and it's like I can't get to the end, can't stop going on about it, like I don't actually want us to talk about anything else all evening.

On my way to the dinner I get my phone out and film the snow falling between the coloured lanterns that hang from some trees. I do it for M. When do I send it? The same evening?

Why does something in me again open to embrace something bad, something threatening, something frightened? As if the frightened part has been forgotten, as if something in me hopes that the threatening part has gone to sleep like a bear in winter, and that now only the thin, sensitive, trembling part, the soft place inside M, will shimmer in front of me? All those times at the kitchen table, the family councils, *This time, if things haven't improved by next week, then . . .* Then what? *Then we're finished.* Everything, everything that was our world, the family, there'd be no more us then. It felt like an impossibility, and yet it frightened me so terribly. It would rescue all hope: things had to improve, *this time* they had to, Mamma just *had to* find a way to answer him that didn't make him angry, didn't make him furious, so that he wouldn't despair and feel like everything was lost, oh, if only she could find a way and answer him, it seemed so simple to me, if only I could step in and help her out, help them both, make things work.

That's how I'd go to bed at night, not knowing, and no one ever came to sit on the bed beside me, no one came and said anything at all, no one, and I would lie there and try to sleep, and there was only one way, the same way always: think about something good (birthday), think about it and hold it tight, don't let the darkness in, but keep looking at the light ahead, no matter how dark it was all around, grip that good thing in both your hands, and don't let go.

And then, after three weeks, something in me opens after all.

11

Judith wonders first if she actually heard anything, she's in the kitchen filling a saucepan, the tap's running, but then the doorbell rings again. Is she going to see who it is? She's not expecting anyone. She goes into the hall and there's someone outside, a moving shadow she sees through the flimsy curtain that covers the pane in the door, or it could be a grizzly bear or a gorilla with steam coming out of its nose.

She opens the door and it's a young man standing there, in jeans and an oversized black hoodie, trainers, straight blond hair swept at an angle across his brow. He's holding a large envelope. Mrs Greco, I'm Matt Dillmann, he says, I've been asked to give you something, and he holds the envelope out towards her. My mom wanted you to have them, he says with a nod in the direction of the street. Judith looks past him, to where a dusty low-slung car is parked, waiting. A woman behind the wheel leans towards them, waves and smiles, an unruly head of red curls makes her face look like that of an animal peering from its burrow. Thank you, Judith says, and takes the envelope from his hand. She smiles and waves back with it at the woman in the car, and Matt Dillmann is already crossing the grass verge. Have a good one, he calls back over his shoulder, opens the car door and gets in (his boyish frame, seamless movements), and then the car pulls away and is gone.

The envelope contains photographs of Myrto, a series of black-and-white images, from the concert hall. She stands in the doorway looking at them.

Why can't you give them to her yourself (Matt wonders), but she's like that, she needs this contact with people, through her photographs, then when it gets to the crux she backs away and sends me in her place, while she sits there smoking, hiding, she's nothing but a goddam lens and I'm her go-between, I'm the thread who must connect her to people, but if I say anything she'll just smile and laugh and afterwards she won't even remember what she said, the words stay outside of her while she slips back into her shell and sits there on her haunches humming to herself, staring at some stupid little flower or something, what do I know.

Three days later Judith presents herself at the concert hall office with the envelope in her hand, she asks who took the pictures. They don't know anyone by the name of Dillmann, and they're not the work of their usual photographer either, because he's male. Judith's told them it was a woman with a lot of curly red hair. But then the girl over by the window looks up from her computer and says it sounds like that woman from the trailer park, only she can't remember her name. She was here asking if she could take photographs at some rehearsals one time, the girl says, but it rings no bell with the other one. Judith asks where the trailer park is and the girl says it's northwest of the city out on Highway 27, forty-five minutes, an hour, she says, and you're there.

Judith doesn't have a car, but there's a bus in the morning and another one back in the afternoon, and so the next day she gets on the bus and finds herself a seat behind the darkened windows having told the driver, who was smoking a cigarette outside, that she wants to go to the trailer park and asked if he knew where it was. Oh, Sunshine Canyon, yes, he said, he'd be sure to drop her off.

She looks out at the city, nothing but ordinary residential streets with houses and gardens. She wonders what she feels, but can't gauge anything. She asks herself what she's doing, going to this place, and can give herself no answer. The woman has seen Myrto and has kept photographs of him, but so what? He's not coming back. She says so to herself. To begin with it was something she said to bring on the pain, to feel how much it hurt, feel the wound in her chest open, and then claw at it, as if to get inside it, to be certain she wasn't skipping anything, that she wasn't cheating herself. He's not coming back. It no longer hurt automatically. She looks out at the trees, cows in a field. At the corner of a house, a tethered dog strains at its rope, barking. She can't hear it, but can see the way it expels its barks using its whole body, as if punching itself inside.

11

Matt is standing on the porch when Judith comes to the door, and he sees her long grey hair, the skirt she's wearing, like something out of *Little House on the Prairie*, she could have been holding a gun. But Matt sees something else too, something more. What he sees are Judith's hands as she steps towards him, they brush against his before grasping the envelope. How soft they are. And then when he looks up at her, it's the way her eyes are too. As if they contain something peculiarly soft and at the same time something gleaming, almost concealed, something watchful and hesitant, like pebbles in water, something secretive, something green that sparkles.

11

He's holding a big glass of chocolate milk, there's a yellow box of Nesquik on the table, and he's sitting with his back against the wall of the trailer. Hi, Judith says, coming towards him, she's been wandering around the trailer park and has seen him now, Hi, Matt Dillmann, she says. Hi, he says, and looks up at her, his hair fallen in front of his right eye, and he traces a thumb along the table's metal edging. Your mom, she says, is she home? But his mom is at work and Judith thinks Matt probably ought to be at school, how old is he, seventeen, eighteen maybe. And she thinks that she ought to be sitting at her sewing machine, what's she doing here, it's so long since she's sewn anything at all, but the thought drifts away from her without leaving an impression, as if she's no longer Judith, no longer the woman she sees seated at the octagonal table in the upstairs room or in the sewing workshop in Milan when she thinks about herself, or at the white illuminated tables in the basement of the opera house in Oslo, she can't see herself. But Meryl Streep is clear to her, she can see Meryl Streep in that film, in pictures she has of her in her head, her clear, bright smile, the happiness she exudes as she steps through the screen door and stands wiping her hands on her apron when she hears Clint Eastwood's truck pull up outside the house.

You want a glass of water?

In Finnmark, we used to come home on a school bus, and when we got off and went up the hill and around the bend and were home, my brothers and me, only the dog would be there to greet us and we'd have two hours on our own, two hours free, before Mamma and Pappa came home from work, and the house was an easy place to be, I'm not sure if my younger brother and I would get ourselves something to eat, I can't remember, puffed wheat with sugar and milk, I don't know, but I know my older brother did, he suited himself, dared to do things none of us was allowed, he would knead a lump of butter together with some sugar and chocolate powder until it was soft in his hand, he would make himself a jam sandwich, very occasionally one with chocolate and hazelnut spread, but that was hardly ever, and he would never, ever drink chocolate milk.

Everything was so tacky in our house. I wanted us to have quality furnishings, in proper materials, a wooden table made out of proper wood, china cups, colours that matched and lines that formed a unified whole, like in the pastor's house and in the homes of some of the teachers I'd been to, or the neighbour's house, Jørgen's mother, a sense for things. It wasn't like that at ours. I've seen photos of Pappa's from before he and Mamma met, it was the early sixties, airy Nordic design, style and feeling, but the two of them together were unable to make a home. We had a red velvet sofa and wall-to-wall needle-felt carpeting, no bare wooden floors in our house, the table in the kitchen was laminated; I didn't know the names for these things then, but I did have this very clear sense of something not being solid and good. And of course it's obvious to me now that if my parents' relationship had been good, if they'd felt good about themselves, then it maybe wouldn't have felt so off with that laminated table, that velvet sofa or whatever, it wouldn't have mattered. And yes, there were book-club books and an encyclopedia and a hire-purchase piano in the living room, there were those things too. But what I wanted was beauty, a beauty that was something else, even if I didn't know what exactly, I just knew it was something else, something other than leather sofas with brown coffee tables in front of them, and the television and the unit, which was brown too, with the framed photos on the shelves, no books, but a clutter of ornaments, and the walls done out in orange or green, the way things were in everyone else's homes, the ones I knew and was used to visiting.

Water, yes! That would be nice!

They sit a while, her glass on the table, he'd gone inside to fetch it, in front of them sand and dry grass, the row of mobile homes, a scruffy white dog comes past, skinny, a black cat asleep under a trailer a bit further away. Judith thinks that Myrto taught her some things, but that she was too slow and has only just taken them in now, afterwards, now that he's no longer here. Like this saying yes to a glass of water, accepting it even though she doesn't know what she wants it for, like coming all the way out here to find this woman who isn't even home, and now she's sat here with the son. She's never seen a trailer park before. With Myrto everything was familiar, their way of talking, or of being quiet, showing consideration. She seldom thought about him being Italian, it's only now, after his death, that she's understood more of what that means, how different they are, Norway and Italy, and yet, even from their separate ends of Europe, they came from such similar places, the books they'd read, the references they shared, Anne Carson and Pipilotti Rist, they inhabited the same world. She sees her hand as it holds the glass, so far away it is. She sees this young man, this boy, Matt, his tight skin, his prominent cheekbones, his eyebrows, it's as if he's powdered them, yellow-white, the freckles on his nose and forehead, pale brown, she hasn't noticed until now, and so small his ear is, almost without a lobe, but she stops herself from looking at the ear canal, the hole leading into his skull.

You wanna come down to the river with me, he asks. He looks at her, but doesn't smile. Yes, says Judith. His eyes remain on her for a moment. Then he picks up the yellow box and his glass, which still has some chocolate milk left in it, and her empty one, and puts them on the floor inside the door of the mobile home, closes the door and locks it. He drops the key into his jeans pocket, his narrow hips, they look new, the jeans, not yet washed, his long slender arms.

They go through the trailer park as if following gridlines, straight on, then to the side, straight on, then to the side again. Here and there, she hears the sound of a TV show. A fat woman with pink earphones sits splayed on a white plastic chair, she bulges out underneath the armrests, her eyes are closed and Judith wonders if she's asleep. They emerge from the rows and there are dusty trees, a slope they descend, bushes, and then a path, and she follows on behind him, he holds the thin branches back so they don't swipe into her face, his hand on the branches, she looks at it, and how pretenceless it is, how young and alive. They carry on walking, two more turns and they're there, a stream running through a channel, and Judith wouldn't ever have called it a river. There's a stillness about the place, as if they're far away from everything, inside a cavity. Judith watches the water, the way it runs between the rocks. Further downstream it widens into a pool, the water there darker, and probably deeper too. Come on, says Matt. His hand as he speaks, as if it's reaching out to her, and they skirt a toppled tree behind which saplings grow, and after that they come to a long, high bench with wooden boxes on top, each box with a mesh front, and Matt goes up and unlatches the first, and Judith stands beside him and sees now that the boxes contain rabbits. She sees his face, his calm expression, and his eyes follow his hand as he reaches into the straw, reaches underneath a yellow-grey belly, and lifts.

In her photography book *Immediate Family*, Sally Mann presents photos of her children taken in the place where they grew up in rural Virginia. The steep, crumbling bank, the dried-up riverbed and parched grass, the heat that makes them drowsy. There are two images in particular of Mann's son Emmett, entitled *Emmett and the White Boy* and *The Last Time Emmett Modeled Nude*. Both are from the river. In the first, Emmett is standing by a tree with the White Boy, he's wearing wet bathing shorts, his arms are moist with droplets of water, and the way he's looking straight at the camera, it's as if his eyes are blocked out by a wall, I can't see into them, I don't know what it is I'm seeing. Perhaps his mother could see more than I can, or perhaps not. Perhaps that's why the pictures work, and when he modelled nude for the last time he's in the river, the water looks thick and oily, the woods are dark and the water quite black along the banks, and here too, his eyes, there's an edge to them, there's something we're permitted to see and there's something else we're absolutely not permitted to see, and it's the line between those two things that makes the image shimmer.

Jørgen, the boy who lived next door to us in Tana, was a year younger than me, and with Jørgen I was permitted to go all the way inside. That's what it felt like, his eyes, it was as if there was a tunnel between us that led into a place of light. Or maybe not light, maybe it was more like an open place, a place that was bare, and at the end of that tunnel I was able to, well, I don't know if I could *see* exactly, but I could definitely *sense* the person Jørgen was. And in that space he *was* the light.

Jørgen sussed out where the Home Guard's ammunition depot was and then broke into the place, I don't know what he did with the explosives he stole, but there was always something volatile about him, he tuned his moped and gave me the fastest ride I've ever had, with no helmet on, down through the valley, Tanadalen, the road snaking between the slender birch. He didn't know who his dad was or if his dad was even alive, his mother lived with someone else. Jørgen had copper-red hair and freckles and once made me believe he'd shaved off all his hair and wore a wig and that when it grew back again his hair would have a completely different colour. Jørgen was dyslexic and proud and hot-headed, and school was a mess for him, but I remember him at the bus stop in the mornings, when we'd be waiting for the red school bus to come and pick us up, and the way he teased me then and wanted me to wrestle him so he could force me down into the snow and sit on top of me and breathe into my face while threatening to press the snow he held packed in his mittened hand into my face, and he came to my house once with a porn mag, *Aktuell Rapport*, there he was outside my window one night knocking on the pane, and he had this supplement too containing *readers' own stories* that he wanted me to stash for him so his mother wouldn't find it when she tidied his room. It was just an excuse, I think he wanted me to read it, and of course I did, and I remember the story about two sisters aged twelve and thirteen and their uncle, and I remember I thought it was completely normal for those kids to be horny and to want to have sex with their uncle, and they went at it *like rabbits*, I remember that was what it said, which puzzled me because I didn't get the connection. More than thirty years later I went to visit Jørgen in prison in Oslo, I saw how angry he was and the way he tried to wrench free when they led him away to search him after visiting time was over, even though he knew the routine, he told me as we sat there together that afterwards they would strip-search him and poke their fingers up his bum, to make sure I hadn't slipped him anything in the way of drugs, he was in there doing time for a thousand different things, all of them I suppose explosive in a way, amphetamine, cocaine, I don't know exactly what he used, only that he was as thin as a rake and wired even there, in the slammer. A few years before that, he sent me something he wanted me to look after, he was a glass-blower by then and had made this yellow jug with a circular hole for a handle, and stemmed glasses, the same yellow, the happiest yellow ever, and he sent me these things and I still have them, in my storage space in the basement of the building where I live in Oslo, and I don't know where Jørgen is now, all I know is that when I was twenty-one and was working in Tana over the summer, someone had left a big bunch of dark red roses outside the door of the flat where I was staying, I was a psychology student in Oslo and had a summer job on the psychiatric ward where my dad used to be the head nurse, and there was no card attached to those flowers, no message, no nothing, but I knew, even though we hadn't seen each other in years, I knew straight away those roses were from Jørgen.

What love is meant to be ours?

Do we see something in the other person, and does the other person (seen, found!) then want us to take care of what we see? A mouth-blown jug, delicate, take this, look after it, keep it for me – so that it won't get lost, so that it doesn't go to pieces? So that something is rescued, so that I don't destroy *myself*.

Judith is allowed to hold the rabbit. She is surprised at the thinness of its belly, it feels as if the rabbit, its whole being, is wide open in her hands.

Afterwards, they walk back up to the trailer park. The light is lower now. She wants to ask Matt about something, she can't remember what. She feels so thankful, as if he's been looking after her a while. Has it got a name, she asks him eventually. What, says Matt. The rabbit, says Judith, what's its name? He looks at her, looks almost angry, she can't understand it. Little Arrow, he says, but then his expression changes, as if he allows it to change, chooses or dares to let go of himself, and he smiles then, it's the first time he's smiled, and there's such a softness in his eyes then, she wants to trace a finger over the softness in him, and reaches out her hand, and he says then that if she's to catch the bus back, she'll have to get a move on, and he's right about that, he indicates the direction, and Judith thanks him, Thank you, Matt. For what, he calls from behind her after she starts to run.

11

I sit writing at the dining table in the living room. Since L died I've sat here rather than at my desk in the study. His piano stands over by the wall with the big portrait of me that he painted for one of my birthdays. I have my books in front of me, the ones I'm reading and the ones that form a kind of landscape around the novel, they're spread out here so I can see them. I sit at the end of the table, and if I lift my gaze I can look out through the window straight ahead. The apartment is high up in the building. Below are the road and the canal, there's quite a way over to the buildings on the other side. Above them I see the rooftops stretching away, and two church steeples, the bells in them ring when evening comes.

There's so much I know but can't understand (about M and me), as Enquist says in *Downfall*, I've just finished reading it again. I don't know how many times I've read it, and I'm already starting to read it again now, because it's so hard to get this novel going, the one I'm working on here. I hadn't written anything since I wrote the short text that became a book when L was ill, and nothing at all after L died. But then I wrote an essay about Vesaas's *Spring Night*, at that point I hadn't written in two years, and what helped me get started was Enquist's *The Parable Book*, which I'd been given as a Christmas present. Most recently I've been reading *To the Lighthouse* again, I'm giving a talk about Virginia Woolf at the library in Bergen after Easter, and now I'm rereading *Mrs Dalloway*, and I've always admired intensely Woolf's swirling flow, as if what she writes is a leaf carried along by a stream, it's the way Christina Hesselholdt writes as well, the two of them are as if related, my aristocratic friends, but I understood when I took *Downfall – Nedstörtad ängel* as it's called in Enquist's Swedish – from my shelf in Oslo and read it on the flight back to Milan that, yes, Woolf is absolutely marvellous, but it's in Enquist's writing that I feel at home. And in fact it's always been that way. It's only now I realise. I always used to feel I was falling short. Because I haven't got that kind of imagery to my prose, the kind Woolf and Hesselholdt have. My words feel a lot more concrete, tangible, *fragments of existence* (as Birgitta Trotzig writes), and I use them to try and discover something I don't yet know. As such, it feels like Enquist's there in the writing too, his presence making it possible for me to ask questions and search for what's important. I first read *Downfall* the year before I started at the writers' school in Bø, where I wrote my first novel, a year before I even realised I was going to write something, I read it then, and it was the photography teacher we had at the art and design school in Oslo who'd talked about it, this was in 1992, when it had only just come out. I'd read so much by Duras at that time, and had thought she was my closest kin, but then Enquist for me was even closer, even deeper. *Downfall*, the way the images scrape against each other, the way there are no transitions or explanations; Pinon, the monster in the cave, who bears on his forehead the head of his beloved Maria; the boy, who has killed two young girls; the stillness in the early hours of morning, which is the novel's *now*; the fog, and the bird rising from the lake. And the fact that it's such a desperate novel, written from such an exposed, near-abandoned place, is something I never really grasped all the other times I read the book. I've been gripped by it, always, but I never realised until now just how anguished it is in its desperation.

It's early afternoon and the sun is already on its way down, a yellow light falls onto the table from directly in front of me, I get up and step over to the window, lower the shutters.

Judith sits in the living room in the green house, on the sofa with a blanket covering her legs, and the room is dusty, she sees it now, how it needs vacuuming and dusting, and the windows could do with a clean as well, but she stays put, on the sofa, and waits.

On the table in front of her lie the photos of Myrto that were taken by Matt's mother. She wishes they'd said more to each other, she and Myrto, that they hadn't been so quiet. But when he was with her it had never felt necessary to say very much, as if they always said more by being quiet together, the way his eyes could sweep over her and open something inside her, making it good to be there with him. What is there to say then? But now that he's not there any more, and unable to look at her, she thinks that if they'd talked she could have thought about what they said. His words would still have been with her now, after he's gone. But she doesn't know if it actually would have changed anything. What would she have done with those words?

The photos are from some rehearsals, Myrto is conducting, and my goodness, how handsome he is, his facial expressions are so vivid, so intense, the tiny shifts in emotion from one image to the next, the way he flows with the music, surging and swirling, so wholly immersed. So unfamiliar he seems to her in those photos. She wishes she could feel the pangs of his absence in her breast, but she can't, the closeness they shared, she can't feel it any more, can no longer feel inside her that the burning fire of a man she sees in those photos was hers, her husband, that they were a couple, together, in their innermost being. She can't feel it any more, what they meant to each other, the way she would cry on her pillow in the mornings and how he would simply gaze at her then, as he lay beside her with his hands under his cheek, not saying anything, but being there with her. And the way everything in his eyes could go astray, especially when he was inside the music, as if he had lost faith in the world and himself, and the way she could see that, and could smile at him then, and the way she could see how it helped, her smile, and her eyes would be like a ledge on a rock face onto which he could manoeuvre himself. Where did it go, Judith wonders, it's all turned to dust, that too, she thinks to herself, and inside me I'm becoming dust.

Who am I now, what life will now be mine, Judith wonders, and she doesn't know.

//

Pappa texts me from Oslo, he follows the war in Ukraine and writes nearly every day to keep me up to date, he wants hope, he says, he can't go on unless there's hope, and he keeps up with the women's football as well, it's the only thing that gives him something else to think about, but today he writes: *If someone loved me – I'd give everything back then – "die, if that be fitter" – the fact of the matter is I wouldn't understand if anyone did "love" me – I've not been that – loveable – it was all imagined – but I'd have done anything at all for whoever did "love" me – it gradually occurs to me that you've tried many times to express that I mean something to you – but that I'm too afraid to acknowledge this – I don't know how a loveable person behaves – but anyway I mean well and am grateful for the life around me – on the plain I'm free from harm and happy – best wishes to you and hope for Ukraine.*

Capable of being loved, is what he means. And *too afraid to acknowledge this* – but Pappa, I was your little girl.

Is it losing someone again that makes you frightened? Or is it opening yourself up, laying yourself bare – the very openness of that? Having that place inside you open, that place that has to do with love and loving and being loved – does it make you feel vulnerable, does it hurt, when that place is wide open to the world? Because that place is what actually is *you*? It's the most precious thing you have. And what if it's not looked after. If someone breaks it. All it takes is a look, a look of contempt. That place being so open, and then the knife of contempt. The slashing knife. And there, dead it lies, barren. That feeling then of it being YOU that's broken. The person you are. When being open then means writhing stark naked on the floor, a hysterical baby unable to touch the bottom, unknowing whether there is one or if everything's just bottomless. And so it's better just to do without. To close down on love. Shut it out, avoid opening yourself up altogether.

But to live a whole life without?

All those evenings with Albinoni on the record player and home-made vodka in his cup, me in my bed downstairs, my brothers in their beds in the adjoining rooms, and I'd lie there listening to his voice grow harder, his anger building up, and eventually he'd snap, and then came the slaps, the punches, the kicks, the shoves, and the sound of all that drifting down the stairs to where we lay, and always they'd have sex in the end, and I could never understand what sex had to do with all those things that hurt so much, but no one ever explained it to me, and there was no one to ask either.

But what's alarming now, for the person in me who drinks herself into oblivion every night, feels like something else, and more, something that's beyond everything, bottomless, and quite unexplainable.

And I so much understand Clarissa Dalloway when she thinks, *Even now, quite often if Richard had not been there reading the* Times, *so that she could crouch like a bird and gradually revive, send roaring up that immeasurable delight, rubbing stick to stick, one thing with another, she must have perished.* And I think about Judith and how this must have been what Myrto was for her, his physical presence in the room, knowing that he was there in the world somewhere, out to lunch or at the concert hall, and that soon, in a very short time, she would hear his key in the door and he would come inside, put the light on in the hall, and before hanging up his coat or taking off his shoes would come all the way up the stairs and stand there on the top step just to look at her at the sewing machine, to look at her with the sky and all the stars in his eyes and say, Hello.

For my eighteenth birthday, Pappa gave me Kierkegaard's collected works, a box set of five paperbacks in different colours published by Gyldendal in Copenhagen. The pages have yellowed, his handwriting too, a hand used to writing, born before the war: *Congratulations on your 18th birthday – from your Father*, as his father too had written in the Bible he gave his son on *his* eighteenth – *from your Father and Mother*, a soft, leatherbound Bible with gilded edges that's followed him from place to place through all his moves, all through his life, all the way to where he's living now, at the top end of Kirkeveien. And it's not because he's read a lot of Kierkegaard, Pappa's dyslexic, but Kierkegaard is in any case a mountain, and Løgstrup too, Løgstrup's *responsibility*, and I haven't read much Kierkegaard either, but I've read *The Sickness unto Death*, and I've read Marguerite Duras's novella whose title is basically the same, and for me they're both about not being able to love, Kierkegaard talks about relating to God, but to my mind it's the same thing, if you love someone then God's in there too somewhere, regardless. In Duras's story a man pays a woman to stay with him in a hotel room for sixteen days, he wants her to teach him how to love. The way I remember it, he's ill and is going to die whether he learns how to love or not, the story has this undercurrent of lurking death.

I'm going to Oslo again, just for one night this time, and I've already arranged with Pappa that I'll come and see him straight from the airport and that we'll watch the news together, and then one morning he texts me: *Shall I take some prawns out of the freezer Tuesday so there's something for you to eat?*

In *Captain Nemo's Library* Enquist writes about two boys born on the same day and then when they're six someone claims they were mixed up at birth and now they've got to be switched back. The varnish on the bedposts of the bed in which the novel's first-person narrator has slept for six years is blistered, and in the darkness of evening, in the light summer nights, the blisters turn into animals, living animals that look after him and speak to him, and he can understand what they say. When the boys are switched back and he finds himself in an unfamiliar household, there are no animals on the bedposts of his new bed. He thinks about them being left behind. Who'll look after them now that he's no longer there?

The girl I used to be: no varnish-blister animals, only an ordinary English Setter that would come and lie down beside my bed at night. It was where she liked to lie, the two of us together on our own, but maybe she was afraid, maybe she too was afraid.

M's world resembles my own from before he was born, the fishing and all the being outdoors, and he's as if melded together with his motorbikes, which reminds me of the snow scooters outside all the houses in Tana Bru when I was growing up. And I think about Pappa's *gamme*, the traditional Sámi turf hut whose handwritten deeds bearing his name he received from an elderly Sámi man who was ill and who died shortly afterwards. No one owns those huts, they're common property, but the duty of looking after one, keeping it in good repair, comes with certain rights in the way of motorised access and fishing, not that I think any of that was important to Pappa, what was important to him was having this special place in the wilderness whose upkeep he was responsible for and which he could feel was his own. *When the Russians come*, he would say to my brothers and me when we were there with him in our camouflaged hats, the netting hanging down from the brim and covering our shoulders to keep the midges away, as if we were at war, and our rucksacks would be dumped outside, and we had fishing rods with us, and the white dog would be zigzagging through the heather further away, this was in the eighties, the Soviet Union still existed, under Gorbachev by then, Khrushchev and Brezhnev were gone, the radio played *I hope the Russians love their children too*, and no one could have known then that one day Putin would be in charge and that it actually would happen, that the Russians invaded another country. *When the Russians come*, Pappa would say, *we'll come here. We'll stay here all through winter.*

His *when* – never an *if*. Pappa was convinced, to him it was inevitable there'd be a war, it wouldn't be safe anywhere, and there'd be nowhere else to hide.

All through winter. The endless winter. The snow. To be alone there in all that white, forever.

At the same time: nature was so unequivocal. The lines of the map were so clear and so long. The hut was such a strong place. The last of the great empty plains, to be ten years old and run the last bit of the way, knowing we were there, our rucksacks slung, a sweeping wind keeping the midges at bay, to run that last bit of the way, to the edge. And to halt there, at the dip in the terrain, the hut nestled among the stunted birch trees by the small lake. The grey ribbon of the river twisting away beyond it, encircling, deep and narrow where the salmon and trout were, and there were grouse too, and the trees threw shade on the banks, branches reaching down, and how much I was reminded of the place, how vividly it came back to me a thousand years later when cycling under a tropical canopy of vegetation with L, on the narrow pathways that followed the river in the Mekong delta, and we'd race down the slope, my brothers and me, our legs would know the way among treacherous roots and soggy bog-holes, and there was something about the basin in which that old hut lay, as if it had been scooped out of the landscape by hand, as if the earth had been scooped away and the hole then patted so there'd be a rear wall, making it a cosy, safe place.

Safe?

Judith cycles through the streets to where the woods begin, she continues along the broad path and people are out walking or jogging, a man with a blue pushchair. At the lake she secures her bike to a tree and crosses the grass to where the floating jetty reaches out across the water. She walks to the end of it, then kneels, as if the jetty were a prayer stool, and then she looks down.

There's something about the way the water moves and reflects the light, as if the crest of every ripple were a hand holding something out to her, then, abruptly, holding something else, changing all the time. There's something delicate about this constant flux, it gives her so many ways in which to think about Myrto.

In Milan there's a little church I go to, by the big canal, on the side that's pedestrianised, the Chiesa di San Cristoforo, it takes me about twenty minutes and I'm there. The church is open all day and even if the canal area's often quite busy with people, it's nearly always empty. It's from the twelfth century and there are still vestiges of the frescoes from the period, or at least from a very long time ago, the interior all earthen colours and dim candlelight, while a Gregorian choir loops from a loudspeaker. I went to that church while L was ill and I've been going there ever since, a good place to set out for a little walk, the long line of the canal makes it easy to think, and then I'll go in and sit down at the back somewhere, there's only seven rows of benches, the altar's an old grindstone resting on an iron frame, a white cloth to cover it, and when I sit down there, nearly every time, without having anticipated it, I start to cry.

I wrote about that in a chat with a girlfriend of mine on Messenger once, when L was ill, that I had a church I went to where I sat and cried, but then after I'd sent it I realised I'd been in the wrong chat and that it hadn't gone out to my friend but to a group chat with Mamma and Pappa, and I felt straight away how wrong it was, how far too intimate a thing it was to tell them about, crying on my own in a church, but this was before you could retract a message, so there was nothing I could do about it, it was sent and that was that.

I copy-pasted what I'd written and sent it to my friend too, and she read it and replied immediately, telling me how important it was to have such a place, and good for you. There was never any reply from Mamma or Pappa.

From my bookshelf in Oslo I take Enquist's *Ett annat liv* (A Different Life). And from the very beginning: how for him there was always a world outside, outside the house, outside the home, a world to which he belonged, to which he was attached and able to write about. His story is rooted in a wider rural community. It wasn't like that for me. For me it was as if everything outside the house was a scenery that could be changed, as if everything outside the house was without any real meaning. Not because what happened inside the house was so important, but because it was so frightening.

Frightening, the whole time. In what way?

Was it the contempt in Pappa's eyes if I said something wrong, if my brothers said something wrong, if Mamma did? Was it when the tone of voice seemed to angle what was said *at* Pappa or what Pappa stood for or what was right and good? You never quite knew what was wrong and what was right until it was too late to correct yourself. Was it wrong to answer quickly and eagerly, or to remain silent and not show off, not be *social*? Astrid Lindgren was right, Anne-Cath. Vestly was wrong. Existentialism and Kierkegaard were right. The Bible was right.

Being frightened underran everything. It was what governed us, but we couldn't ever talk about it. We had to pretend it didn't exist.

We couldn't forge alliances, my brothers and me, we couldn't afford to, we were mercenaries in the service of our own survival, disloyal, committed to nothing but getting by, a moment at a time.

Why are we so frightened when Pappa is angry?

I can ask myself that now that I'm fifty-three and Pappa's a brittle twig of eighty-seven shuffling across the floor.

Why this trembling fear still, in this adult body of mine, when it's forty years since I lay in that bed listening to the kicks and blows, would it be tonight, Mamma dead and Pappa in prison, foster homes for me and my brothers, and would they let me keep the dog?

The red notebook we take turns to write in, my brothers and I, when the family council meets, once a week, once a fortnight, we lay down a plan, what we're going to have for dinner, pancakes, fried trout, the brothers to do the dishes Tuesday and Thursday, and my job's to do the bathroom and clean the toilet, and pancakes and trout and dishes are surface words, what they really say is *I'm so afraid I'm so afraid I'm so afraid I'm so afraid* and then it starts, you can hear it in Pappa's voice, and Mamma just sits there and the tears start running down my little brother's face and they're crocodile tears, Pappa says, and the hardness builds up in his voice and then the tone is there inside my head, it takes me away through the window and out towards the lines and the light and the river that we can't see but which lies there like a crease in the landscape, a cut, running and running towards the sea.

There is no tone inside my head to take me away, I sit there on my chair the whole time, I stare and stare at Pappa because I'm Lindgren's Ronia, and Karl too, I'm his little girl and he needs me, Pappa, it doesn't matter how much he frightens us, he needs everything I have. And I can write this now, but I didn't think it at the time, I don't know what I thought then, I didn't think at all, I just was. Alone in all the Frightening.

When I started university, sociology at first, I couldn't take it seriously: it was so sedate, all those concepts you just had to learn. Pappa of course had talked about sociology at our round tables, but that was different, it wasn't the concepts I was focused on then, it was Pappa, his voice, what he was actually saying. What was important was always something else. University: surely that had to be something More. There had to be something Hidden. Anyway, the way I trip over my feet when I go down the stairs in the morning with my exercise mat under my arm on my way to the gym and the Egyptian concierge calls out to me from the courtyard where he's sweeping up, *Ciao cara*, and it makes me jump.

As if meeting Matt was something that already happened in the winter. Long before he rang the doorbell and was standing there with the photos. That winter Judith spent alone in the green house as if she was some little figure, a doll, moving through the rooms, and those grand proportions, the height of the ceilings and the imposing windows, the bay windows, the ocean-like sofa, the rugs, the way she could get up in the living room and go all the way through to the table in the kitchen. As if she's just a child wandering about in that house all on her own. There's no one else there. No one calls. A thin grey light from the windows, stronger where the sun comes in, from different angles as the day goes on. Where is Matt, then, in all this? There – in the gossamery, thin, soft parts. The parts that are almost impossible to see. In Judith looking out at the grass in front of the house after it's snowed. The snow is so quiet. Something of Matt is already there.

When it happened, tangibly: the phone call from the concert hall, and she puts on a light jacket and her shoes and picks up the phone charger and wraps the cord around her fingers and tucks the end in so it lies snugly in her pocket, she tries to think of what she's going to see, but the only images that come to her are from films, wheeled stretchers made of steel and flashing red ambulance lights in the night, only it's not night, it's afternoon, just before four o'clock, and she wonders whether to take a book with her, she even knows which one, *What Artists Wear* by Charlie Porter, because it's easy to dip in and out of, she thinks, if she takes that one she'll be able to be with Myrto and with herself as well. Is there anything else she ought to take? As if she's going away on a long journey somewhere and had better have something to eat with her – but at the same time: the fact that she can't move quickly enough – arms twenty feet long, to reach from the hallway into the kitchen, into the fridge, to snatch up a yoghurt, and what about a spoon? No, Judith, get going. And then out the door, and the next thing she remembers is going under the trees and not being sure if she locked the door or not, but she can't go back now, all she can do is hurry along underneath the tall trees, and there are gaps between all things, a gap between her thoughts and this situation of Myrto being taken to United Hospital, she can't join them up, establish contact. She walks as fast as she can along the American sidewalk with its green grass verges, Dayton, delightful Dayton, Judith thinks to herself, Judith! Imagine walking here and finding pleasure in the trees when something just happened to your husband that might possibly change everything forever. She tries to sense the drama of it, but can't, she feels nothing, only a kind of tension, something action-packed.

By the time she goes past the cathedral that feeling has gone, everything now opens out towards downtown and the trees no longer give anything soft, there are no trees, there is no protection, there are the skyscrapers in the distance and everything feels raw, like putting your hand directly to a wound, she turns right through the underpass, the freeway above her, the rumble of traffic, and then she's there, at the hospital. My husband, she says at the reception desk, and a bald black man in a bright purple hospital uniform appears and without smiling says, Come with me, and she does, she follows him into the lift, they go up a few floors and then step out and go down a corridor, round a corner and through a door, and then at last she's there, at Myrto's bedside.

//

There's a Netflix documentary Emma Cooper made about Marilyn Monroe and the first thing you hear in the film is Marilyn's own voice, which wraps her words in softness, and this softness is *her voice*, the voice of Marilyn Monroe, softening the words so that they don't feel hard or sharp to the listener, and *why was it necessary* for Marilyn to talk like that, to issue her words in such a soothing voice, a voice that says: I wish you no harm. There is no harm in me.

Later, there's a bit where she's talking about when she was growing up, and says: Happiness isn't something I ever took for granted. She stayed with ten different foster families before spending two years in a children's home, then with an appointed guardian, her mother was in a mental hospital. She says that when she was put in the children's home she would say to people: I'm not an orphan. Every woman she'd see, she'd say, There's a momma. Every man she'd see, There's a daddy. Marilyn was married for nine months to baseball star Joe DiMaggio, who beats her up in their hotel room while she's filming that movie with the skirt scene, her white skirt billowing around her thighs as she stands over a subway grate, and the photo showing her bare thighs is pinned up on walls all over America, he beats her up and Marilyn said she screamed and yelled for us, her hairdresser says, *but we couldn't hear her through those thick walls, you know*, and the interviewer asks if Marilyn was left bruised or with black eyes, and the woman says no, it was more on her shoulders, but with a little make-up she was back on set and went ahead and worked.

DiMaggio with his big triangle of a nose, and it was the only time Marilyn cried, or not cried exactly, but you can see it in her eyes, there's a press conference, all the photographers and the microphones, when the divorce was made public.

He understood some things about me. And I understood some things about him, Marilyn says. What was it they understood? What wounds of hers bled against his, chafed and seeped and bled, what was it they recognised in each other that no one else but they could?

And so we're standing there in front of the one we love or whatever, the one we recognise ourselves in, and what if the adult in us then falls away and it's the child left standing there, the child in us and the child in that other person, and what if we can't help that child because the child is only a child, in you and in me, and what do we do then. What can we do.

The movie tells us Marilyn didn't have many friends, *I like people, but I don't have many friends*, it seems like she drifted among other people, her last therapist (there are interviews with his wife, his son and his daughter, the therapist himself died not long after Marilyn) believed she had need of a sense of belonging and he tried to treat her by making her a part of his family, he invited her into his home, so they all got to know her, and they and everyone else who's interviewed, everyone liked her, they all talk about her with such warmth, it's that softness in her voice, the light in her that shines even in the childhood photographs, black-and-white images of a chubby little Marilyn smiling, yes, smiling even as a very, very small child, regardless of *happiness isn't something I ever took for granted.*

And this: *When it's afternoon and there's a break before the evening's performance, and he comes in through the door, and sometimes then they would lie on the sofa together and look at each other, and it was like being held by something soft, as if there was a big hand underneath them, holding them both up.*

It's long after that, towards the very end. How does it connect with *after that day, that birthday, that point was a place she tried to avoid*? Avoid his anger, the weak point in that other person, like the bog-hole into which the foot sinks in the soggy mire without finding a hold, avoid putting your foot there, in that spot you sense is weak, is that it? How safe is what's safe anyway? Is there actually any rest, any sense of security anywhere?

M takes me with him to Mont Blanc, we get the cable car and wander about up there like it's the moon, but the important thing is not our spectacular dangling in the air, the important thing is something else, seemingly unremarkable, which is that M drives up a lane in one of those small mountain villages and pulls up outside a house of grey stone and leans forwards, looks up at the house and says, Here. As if he's already told me everything, but he hasn't, maybe in his head he has, but not to me, I've no idea where we are. What do you mean, I ask. This is where I lived, he says, with the old couple who looked after me, he says. We get out and step over the wall and go up the slope into the little garden, the shutters are closed, it's empty. I try to picture him, his mother getting into the car down by the road and waving to him, her little boy standing on the grass. We go back down. He drives a bit further on and stops by a field. He lets the dog out, we go through a barrier and follow a gravel track that winds its way upwards, the sun's shining. We say nothing, M smokes, he glances sideways at me, smiles, a pleasant, boyish smile. After a short while we turn round and go back. All of a sudden he wants to have sex, we'll do it in the car, he says, and we never do it in the car. We walk back and let the front seats down and I lie back and sort of grip his arms while he takes me, while he sort of clings to me and can't get deep enough inside me, can't hold me tight enough, not ever.

//

you wanna come down to the river with me, asks Matt Dillmann, his hand there on those branches

//

The trees are greening up, Judith goes towards downtown along Dayton and there are the driveways of the houses, the cars standing parked, what must it be like to come from here, she wonders, American, with this as your authentic starting point, not just something you've seen in films.

A friend sends a video message, his latest relationship left him needing help from a crisis centre, and I watch it while Judith's out walking, he's at home in Norway and I can see that he's wheeling a pushchair with one hand while talking into the camera, so it must be grandfather's day, and he's so very small in that little iMessage window, like in that installation by Pipilotti Rist where she has this room full of handbags on plinths and when you go up and look into one there's a little sphere inside, and inside that sphere there's a tiny woman talking up at you in a little voice, a whisper, so you've got to put your ear close, and she's telling you something, I can't remember what, just that feeling of being entrusted with a secret.

Reaching the cathedral, where the trees come to an end and the road slopes away down the hill, Judith pauses.

Everything is so open.

Open, inside her too. Empty. Where are you, Myrto, she asks inside herself. No reply. What now?

She got old with Myrto. She met him when her menstruations were petering out, it was with Myrto she sat and sweated in the mornings as they drank their coffee on the sofa, her pyjamas would be wet through, and after another year the way her skin got thinner, her hair too. In the four years she was with Myrto she started down that pathway to being old. And then all of a sudden he was just gone, and now she's here, and she can't really use the word *hurled* – as in hurled into this place on her own – because to be hurled is to be thrown in a certain direction, but there's no direction in this, and no momentum, it's more like she's been let go of. Something, whatever it may be – life? – has let go of her, like a hand that was holding her tight and then just opened. Abruptly, the way Thumbelina is popped from inside the flower, she finds herself far from home in America's vastness, and the life she lived with Myrto, driven on by the *we* of their togetherness, is no more. It simply no longer exists. The palms of her hands ache as she thinks of this, as if her own hands had been holding it all, and now it's not there any more.

But there's this as well: that she just doesn't know. She doesn't know what there would have been otherwise. She hasn't the strength for anything. Sewing? What, then? Walk downtown? Why? Go back?

I think about *Twilight*, the vampire movie my daughter watched when she was fourteen, fifteen years old, I watched it with her, lay down on the bed beside her and watched how they transformed themselves and could move through the air in a split-second, their pale, sincere faces, the vampire Edward and Bella, who's human, he with the regal name and she with the surname Swan, which has that ring of Proust, from deep inside the forests of North America, and it's their sincerity as well as the forces they possess, their strength and speed, that make me think about that film now, because Edward and Bella are so much in love with each other, but there's so much death in their connection, her blood is what can keep him alive, but if he drinks her blood, she'll die. It's serious stuff. They're so vital to each other and yet so mortally dangerous too.

The way Bella can wake up in the middle of the night and Edward's just *there.* Imagine if things were like that in real life. Imagine Judith, standing there on the sidewalk, the road sloping away and Minneapolis's skyline in front of her, the Mississippi flowing through its channel, and then Myrto just *appearing* at her side. If only in a flash. He looks at her, they see each other, he touches her arm. *Don't be afraid.* Is that what he says? Is that the message he brings, before instantly he's gone again, vanished into a different time dimension than the one we take to be real?

Don't be afraid.

Is that what love is?

No werewolf appears where Judith stands on the sidewalk, no vampire materialises, not even a common or garden plumber, but then someone says Hi, and when she turns round it's Matt, the envelope guy, trailer-park guy. Hi, she says, where did you come from? Hi, he says again, and smiles, his blue eyes are like gleaming slits filled with gold, and they stand there like two awkward teenagers, though he's the only one who's actually a teenager, she's thirty years older, Hi, Judith says again, hi.

Matt plays the organ in the cathedral, the regular organist is teaching him, and this afternoon, since there's nothing else going on in the church, he's got practice and asks if she'd like to go inside with him. And so Judith goes inside the cathedral, she says hello to the organist and it turns out he knew who Myrto was, he offers his condolences. She takes a seat halfway down the nave, in the enormous interior, and after a few moments the organ bursts into life and she lets its thunderous waves pass through her, such a tremendous sound produced by such a skinny, boyish frame, and she feels how the bench softens underneath her thighs, she thinks of Matt's back, his neck, so slender and clear to her as he went back across the verge to his mother's waiting car, regal.

M knows nothing about classical music, he doesn't know who Roald Dahl is either, whose books L translated, he's never heard of *Matilda* or *The Witches* or *Charlie and the Chocolate Factory*, and he still hasn't read *Mio, My Son*, and when we talk I often think it's as if language isn't that connected to things in his world, whereas in mine everything's all about capturing something in words, getting it *said like it is*, it's as if he often just plucks his words from a tree without thought, without really looking at them.

At the same time, there's no one who can be as honest, or as precise, as M. When he really feels something, he'll say what it is without hesitating, and there's no two ways about it then, what he says hits home. Like with my drinking. Because it's true that I've been drinking a lot in the evenings. It started when I met the professor, the autumn my daughter turned seventeen, that was when I started getting drunk in a way I'd never done before, I *lost control* of myself, lost my grip, let go, whatever's the right way to say it, but before that it was something I never did, as in never.

I fell in love with the professor too in a way I'd never done before. Well, actually that's not quite true because the year before I met the professor I fell in love with an Argentinian writer I met at the book fair in Paris, but after five days he went back to Buenos Aires and that was the last I saw of him. I was in love with him in a sick, sapless sort of way which I understood had a lot to do with me and very little to do with him – I barely knew the man – but whether I understood that or not, I was so infatuated with him that all I could do was cry and carry on spelling my way slowly through his thick novel in Spanish, which I actually didn't like that much, and I sent him emails and he didn't reply, only the once did he reply, and angrily, because he believed I'd said something about *the way he was* and he made it clear to me in no uncertain terms that he wasn't having it, and it definitely wasn't meant like that, but I couldn't very well send him another email to explain.

Afterwards, I've thought of it as a kind of spring thaw, that infatuation, that it was very convenient for me to be able to attach myself like that to someone living on the other side of the globe who'd always be asleep when I was awake and who I'd never, ever run into or have to relate to in any physical reality ever again. I could make do with playing the whole thing out in my mind, which is where I've lived the greater part of my life anyway, and I looked at his little photo on the flap of the books I'd had the Spanish publisher send me in Oslo, his unruly hair and wonky teeth, as if he was quite as beautiful and clever, as sensitive and as fine as Pappa in the photos that were in that shoebox.

A year later it was the professor and he was Norwegian and moved after a while to Oslo, only a few minutes from my flat, and thereby it all got very physically possible and yet never exactly real, and that was how that was too, a relationship that mostly played out in my mind. Still, I was very much in love with him and I think it must have been in the space between what we had and what I was longing for that I started drinking. I opened myself up to that longing, for someone to open their arms and hold me, and the drinking was a way of dulling or softening the fact that it wasn't happening. Well, I don't actually know, not really. Was I drinking to block out what I was feeling, regardless of what it was? All I know is that for some time now I've been drinking myself into oblivion every night.

And then he had to go and DIE? is what Judith thinks to herself as she sits there in the cathedral listening to Matt Dillmann play the organ, and it's as if the music has taken her by the throat and slammed her up against the wall, she can hardly breathe, she can't get away, and *he just isn't here any more.*

And then, the fact that it's in the thin parts, where the music doesn't insist, but almost lets go and can barely be heard, that his presence is at its strongest, that thinness, that softness, a touch that almost isn't there, and that's when orgasm comes too, not in the hard thrust, but in the letting go, that's when it thickens and becomes unbearable.

//

I'm going up the stairs with my exercise mat under my arm when the lift door opens and I turn round to see that it's M's parents, his mother with a carrier bag and make-up on, a very good-looking woman, we're nearly the same age, and then his father too, or stepfather, with his sparse sandy hair, he's well past seventy and thick-bodied, like an overstuffed sausage, he steps out behind her, and I feel the muscles of my upper arms tense, I bumped into him the day before outside the main door and it was the same then too, I don't know what it is, it's just the *feeling* I get from him, and it's not a good feeling, it's as if he's displeased about something, or is it contempt, something pent up inside him, an anger that can only sizzle and spit, and Camilla says she still sees him calling people out in the street, people who've parked in the wrong place or made a hazardous turn, whatever, ordinary people going about their business, Camilla says, and shakes her head. M's told me he used to take a leather whip to him when he was growing up, I don't know how old he would have been then, but M says it stopped when he was fourteen or fifteen, he just turned on him one day and said, This stops now, and I tell him that's terrible and just thinking about it hurts, to think of little M, his father standing over him with a whip, but M says he needed it, he was a tearaway and out of control, if they hadn't put their foot down and set some boundaries and brought him back into line, his life could have gone horribly wrong, because I'm not just this nice guy you see all the time, M says, and fixes his eyes on me.

And my paternal grandmother, my *farmor*, used to hit Pappa when he was growing up, at the back of the barn at Ørsta with switches of birch, it was pants down and bend over the chopping block, and the mare would stand watching, Pappa says, she'd dish me out a good thrashing. Pappa's told me he was angry with her for a good many years, but eventually they had a talk and straightened things out. Farmor died when I was four. There are very few photographs of her, but I've got one taken in the upstairs sitting room at Ørsta where she lived with my *farfar* when they were old, my uncle had taken over the farm and lived downstairs with my aunt and all my cousins, and Farmor is seated at the table, nurse, missionary and member of the local council, sole provider all those years, from before the war until afterwards, while Farfar was in a Japanese prison camp in China, on her own with the farm, with Pappa and his brothers and sisters, eight in all, the ninth died early, Pappa was the next youngest and she thrashed him, only him.

Eventually Pappa's siblings told her she had to stop, and that was when she stopped, Pappa says. How old was he then? The swish of the birch on his bare backside, the stinging pain, Pappa crying, and Farmor telling him, *Don't you cry*.

Farmor, my paternal grandmother, at the table in the upstairs sitting room, and there's something so hard about her eyes, I can only glance at them whenever I look at that picture.

How do we know who's going to turn out to be violent, the lecturer asks – it's a lecture on the theory of knowledge, part of the compulsory philosophy course, and we're crammed into a narrow lecture hall in the Eilert Sundt building. No one responds, the students are silent and there's a tension in the air, or is it just me, it's the only question I remember from my entire time at university, and eventually I put my hand up and say, *If you were a victim of violence yourself*... and I remember him, the lecturer, looking at me as if in disbelief, as if only then I'd become visible to him, *Yes*, he says. Yes. And how is it that I possess that knowledge, I've betrayed myself, and at the same time it's as if all of us who know what it's like to have that sort of thing going on at home, it's as if suddenly there's a connection between us in that room, for the briefest of moments, I don't know who any of the others are, but I do know that they exist, and at that exact point in time we gaze into that thing together, that thing which is clear to us, at the very front of our days, afraid to death, silent and radiant.

Downtime, M and I have planned a few days away at a place his family owns in the south. I've never been there myself, but M loves it, he's always so cheerful when he gets back, a stony place with sun-scorched trees, and there's the olive harvest, and beaches where he goes fishing, big, wide open spaces, and he's cheerful the way Pappa used to be cheerful when I was little and we were up on the fell, free and light, far away from everything that weighs upon a person and presses them down.

That's the plan, but it all goes awry the night before, it's the same every time: my drinking sends M into a rage and he frightens me. Is that how it starts? Or has it already started by not having stopped, not yet having subsided after the last time – am I drinking now because I'm already afraid? And before I know it I'm biking home with my helmet on, through the streets in the dark, along the canal, I go in through the main door, I go up the stairs and into my apartment and lock the door behind me, and then I'm on my own again, completely on my own and safe.

A couple of days pass and he makes a new plan for us, a shorter getaway this time, three nights in Rome where I've hardly ever been, and he wants to take me there to make amends for things going wrong the last time, and again it's the night before, a Tuesday night, and we're leaving in the morning first thing, a six o'clock start.

I'm having a glass of wine with a girlfriend, waiting for M to come and pick me up, it's one of the first evenings in spring that the sun's been out and we're sitting outside at a pavement café, I drank a beer at home beforehand, and a glass of wine turns into three, M texts me around nineish and I go home to get my things, I'm all packed and ready, clothes and other necessities, a paper bag with a bottle of prosecco and some red wine for the first night in the apartment he's booked, and when he rings the buzzer from downstairs to say he's waiting, I take the lift down with all my stuff and when I step out into the street M appears from round the corner where he's parked and he reaches a hand out for me to give him my bag, but he doesn't look at me, doesn't smile, it's less than a week since last time I biked home from his and he still hasn't softened, and then the paper bag with the bottles in it tears and I see Camilla and her boyfriend coming towards us from the other side of the street and in order for the bottles not to fall out of the bag I sort of sag at the knees with the bag in my lap, and then M appears from round the corner again and he sees me squatting there and he sees Camilla too, and her boyfriend, and he takes the torn paper bag and holds out his hand and helps me to my feet, his face is hard, I smile and wave to Camilla, but then we're already back round the corner and inside the van and on our way and he's not saying anything, just staring straight ahead, and this is the night before we're going to Rome together, this is how it is, and it keeps on like this as we carry the stuff up into his flat, my bag and the things I've brought with me from the fridge, and I go over and put the food items and the bottles on the worktop in the kitchen while M sits down on the sofa with his laptop to finish drawing up a tender for a contract before we go to bed, I can see him from the kitchen and I pour myself some wine from the bottle I opened at home and brought with me, and because I haven't eaten, and because everything, just being there, is so painful, I start chopping some courgette, M's so angry and it makes me so afraid, but he's not saying anything, so it's like I'm there on my own with just my fear, and he doesn't start on me, but it's there the whole time right in front of me, and the rings on the cooker are safety-locked and normally you just have to touch the lock symbol, only it doesn't matter how many times I try I can't get it to work and I pick up the pepper grinder and throw it against the wall and it lands on the hob, though without doing any damage, because I didn't throw it very hard, I wasn't intending to break anything, but I did throw it, and why did I do that, I never throw things, and so M gets to his feet and comes towards me and touches the lock symbol with his finger and the lock releases straight away and he goes back and sits down, and I don't know which one of us speaks first, but me throwing the pepper grinder at the wall has taken the lid off things and M stares at me, angrier now than I've ever seen him before, Angry? You want to see me angry? he says, and he says this several times, his voice gets louder each time, louder and harder, You really, really want to see me angry? and even writing this I feel my legs stiffen, my thighs, my calves, stiffening completely, now, at last, it comes, this is what I've been so frightened about, and now it's steaming towards me, hurtling and rampaging, and I'm so afraid, but now it's in plain sight, everything before was just him being angry, without it coming out, into the open, and I never knew what to do or say, there was never anything concrete I could *react against*, but this, this is plain and clear, and now, this time, the fear I feel is greater than any of those other times, and now I react, I gather my things,

I've already changed into my pyjamas, but there's no time to change back, they'll just have to do, I want out of here now, out, I want never to come back, I pack my things together with a strange clarity, I remember my gym clothes in the sleeping area upstairs, and the make-up I'd brought to keep here in his bathroom, everything, only I haven't got my bike because he picked me up in the van, we were meant to be going to Rome, and he gets up from the sofa and says, I'll take you, and so that's what he does, I put my coat on over my pyjamas and we carry everything out into the van and he drives me back to mine and helps me take everything inside before turning round and leaving, and I go up in the lift, I lock the door of the apartment behind me, and after that I'm on my own, all on my own, home again.

I can't stop it, *see me angry, you really want to see me angry*, it's like it's out there now, the anger, everywhere, it's Pappa upstairs in the living room and Mamma running down the stairs, it's him sitting on top of her with his hands around her throat, an escalation, bare and exposed, and I don't know what's actually happening, what's actually now and is real.

Somewhere in all this we fought, he doesn't want a woman who slumps on the pavement, I tell him Camilla's my friend and she doesn't care if or where I happen to slump, but it's not Camilla, M says, No, of course it's not, I reply, it's your fucking family, you don't want me doing it in front of where *that fucking family of yours* lives, he still hasn't told them about us, he still performs his little charade of going all the way downstairs and back out onto the street after he's had dinner at his aunt's, before coming back inside to see me, because you'd rather have a girl like *her*, I say, the one in that video the mother of a girl he knows sent him, as if she was some kind of a pimp, her daughter in the Jacuzzi with her tits ballooning out of her bikini, he said he thinks she's not half bad, that he used to fantasise about being with her, a fit little Albanian with lip filler and long nails, and when I haven't been drinking and I'm not afraid, that video just tucks away into the place I've got for things that are way below my dignity, come on, if he really wants a thirty-year-old plastic fuck doll to give him a hard-on then as far as I'm concerned he can just get on with it, because it's so far beyond everything I am and everything I want, so far beyond everything I can even imagine having to be compared to, so just GO, do you hear me, GO, that's what I think to myself when I'm not absolutely scared stiff, when I haven't been drinking, when I'm not feeling so utterly wretched about there not being anything good whatsoever in any of this.

Because wasn't it supposed to be *the two of us*, even if he is seventeen years younger, weren't we supposed to try and make a go of this? Get something together, make something beautiful? Weren't we supposed to get up early in the morning and go to Rome?

But it's things that are deeper inside us too, inside him and inside me, things that have been there for some time and that I've gradually become more and more aware of, like the way he kicks his dog, not hard, but rather often, as if he finds it funny, a game of some sort, only it's not funny, and she cowers, the dog, and why does he do that, she means everything to him, he's had her twelve years and organises his time around her, when he's at work from early in the morning he pays someone to come during the day and take her for a walk, so no, it's not funny, and I've been afraid of him for a long time now, I realise when I think back, that for quite some time now I haven't looked forward to seeing him.

The next day, we've cancelled the Rome getaway, M phones and says he wants to come and see me. My legs stiffen, my thighs, my calves, I don't know if I dare let him in, I imagine everything smashed to pieces, the furniture, that he's going to hit me, maybe it'd be better to meet him outside somewhere. He says he's only got an hour, why does he say that, I know he's not working today, he's got nothing else on, he was meant to be away and told everyone. And then he comes, his slender boyish frame steps in through the door, his big smooth head, his glasses, he's brought the shoes I forgot, and my MDMA, we were going to do it together in front of the fire in his family's house in the south, only we ended up not going, and we didn't go to Rome either, and I thought when he phoned that I wasn't going to see him again, so I told him I wanted the MDMA so I could take a trip on my own, at some future time.

He's weighed the crystals and divvied them up into flat little packets of tin foil, a hundred milligrams in each, and put them in a little jar with a lid on, I picture him sitting on the sofa, hunched over the coffee table, weighing and so on, folding the little packets, and he hands me the jar, his arm outstretched, avoiding my gaze. He sits down in the armchair and it's so far from there to the sofa, so I take a stool and sit closer, in front of him, and he starts talking.

It's my drinking, it's too much for him, it's ruining everything and he wants out. He goes on, but it's the same thing he's repeating, and I say, Yes, I hear you, and still he goes on, harder this time, and I no longer know what he's saying, it's not that we're arguing, it's just him going on, and I listen to him for an hour without saying anything, he just goes on and on, and when at last he gets up to leave I go out into the hall with him, and just before he goes through the door I step forwards and hug him, and he hugs me back, we stand there holding on to each other, and I can feel him trembling. His back trembles against my hand, his abdomen trembles against mine, as if there's something inside him that's very small and afraid, something completely other than the hard voice in the living room, so frail it is, so totally vulnerable there, against my body, until then he pulls away and I see that his eyes are red, his cheeks are moist, tears are running from his eyes, and then he turns and is gone.

If we hadn't hugged I might never have seen him again. It would have been left there dangling, *you really want to see me angry*. But this was something else, this was his body, his body in my hands, this *was him*, the man I was in love with and had been right from the start, because everything can be seen in him, his vulnerability so very apparent, like putting your finger to an eye that doesn't shut, touching that moist flickering orb which *is* simply life.

11

Is Myrto there, in the music? Is he there in those sonorous tones, the crashes of sound that emanate from the cathedral organ in St. Paul, Minneapolis, where Judith sits with eyes closed listening to Matt Dillmann as he plays, and she can no longer sense where her body comes to an end, it's as if she is unbounded, as if she is inside the sound, which now and then hurts, so powerful it is, and within those points in time there are no nuances, and in a way no sound either, only the pain of its might, no melody, no continuation or narrative of any kind, and perhaps that's where Myrto is, Judith thinks, in every such point, and *why don't you come to me then, if this is where you are?*

And Myrto does come. From behind the altar he emerges in vestments, he spreads his arms, palms held aloft, and stands before the altar rail with eyes closed as if waiting for something, listening, something in the music, a sign of some kind, and then he opens his eyes and he looks at her and there is peace in his gaze, and tenderness, and without speaking he raises his arms in the blessing, Go in peace, *but I don't want to go*, something in Judith says, howls, screams, *I don't want to go anywhere without you*, listen to me, but Myrto remains standing and a light then surrounds him, or shines from inside him, yellow at first, growing in strength, orange now, then waves of pink that shimmer towards her, glowing, radiating from within him, penetrating her, persisting, sustaining, and it feels like forever, only it isn't forever, because then it thins, the colours wash and fade and are as if drawn inside him again, and eventually there's only light, and the light turns white around him and everything then is white, and he is gone.

Myrto, a voice calls out inside her, Myrto, my Myrto, *Myrto come back to me.* But he does not come back.

Lady, as they call her, played by the Italian Anna Magnani in the 1960 film *The Fugitive Kind*, twice loses the man she loves in a fire. Two men, first her father, when she's still young, her Italian father who has established a vineyard in the Deep South, in Two Rivers County, Mississippi, a place to which young lovers come in order to be on their own in the evenings in summer, torched by vigilantes in retribution for the father having sold alcohol to some black men, and the father perishes in the blaze, which destroys everything, he dies in his efforts to quell the flames. And then again right at the end of the film, when at last another man has come into her life, a man she loves and with whom she has become pregnant, at last *she bears fruit* (with Marlon Brando, the much younger, guitar-playing wanderer in his trademark snakeskin jacket), and there, in the dry-goods store she runs from the old winter garden, where the two of them plan to open a tearoom, he too perishes, the place is set on fire by Lady's dying husband, who also set fire to her father's vineyard. (And he shoots Lady too, with a pistol, and she doesn't survive.)

In her essay 'Hållpunkter, hösten 1975' (Reference Points, Autumn 1975) Swedish writer Birgitta Trotzig states: "The main problem is dismayingly simple. A quick dash from birth to death. That the human world ought to be a community of love. Why is it not?"

In Pasolini's *Mamma Roma* from 1962, the same Anna Magnani plays an ageing prostitute who has finally managed to save up enough money to buy a flat on the barren outskirts of Rome and can now offer her young son a better life. She sets up selling vegetables at a market and strives to give the boy everything he wants, nothing is too much, a gramophone, she even scrapes together to buy him a motorcycle, but then it all comes apart, it's hard to say exactly what goes wrong, why can't her son accept that she's now there for him and wants to give him everything she has, her warmth, her devotion, her nearness, why does it go so wrong, he ends up arrested, strapped to a cot in the jail, and there he dies, on that cot, as if crucified.

Tennessee Williams wrote the screenplay for *The Fugitive Kind* and at one point, well into the film, not long before the store is set on fire, Magnani gives Brando a palm leaf. She tells him it's blessed, and after that events quickly unfold towards a repeat of the previous violence, a repeat of the previous blaze, a repeat of the destruction of that which carries inside it new life, the softness of new possibilities. *Mamma Roma* contains no explicit religious motif – there is no *pietà* in plain sight – and yet the religious aspect feels so close at hand, so apparent. And when in 2012 Marlene Dumas sets out to paint the mother of Christ for an exhibition at Milan's Stelline gallery, she experiments with various models, among them Pasolini's own mother, who plays the older Maria in his *The Gospel According to St. Matthew*, but is dissatisfied with them all, she feels the work is thwarting her. Not until she paints Anna Magnani's face in mid-scream at the point in the film when the son, Ettore, fails to come home and his mother realises she'll never see him again, her beloved only begotten son, not until Dumas paints the scream on the face of the prostitute mother does Maria, Mary, become real.

Everyone liked Marilyn, the softness in which she wrapped her words, the voice of Marilyn, *adding* something, and why did she do that? Is she saying: don't hit me? Is that what the voice says? Softness as a counterweight, a manoeuvre, an extinguisher of hardness to come?

Marilyn receives the David di Donatello award for Best Foreign Actress of 1958 at the Institute of Italian Culture in New York, and since Anna Magnani also happens to be filming in America, she is called upon to congratulate Marilyn. Their two faces beside each other, Anna's and Marilyn's, and in a way it's only when Magnani appears that Marilyn becomes apparent, Magnani stepping in from the wings with dark rings under her eyes, without make-up, not done up in any way, she seems so *real*, unlike Marilyn, who of course is just as real, only real in a different reality, there's a layer to Marilyn that Magnani lacks, Marilyn is dazzling white, her hair is styled, the neckline plunging, she smiles and blinks and licks her lips, *but not in any false way*, it doesn't come across as coquettish, it just seems like it's all she can do, to do her best, or is it the other way round, that *this* is what she does, this is what she's learned so very well, far too well, long before she knew she was learning anything at all, brave little Marilyn, putting herself out in a version that made both herself and the situation she was in as *unassailable* as possible, and it's only in the few seconds where the microphones aren't working and they have to start again that something else becomes apparent, for a moment she looks desperate, or lost, as if now she's clinging to a script, and then, when things don't proceed like they're supposed to, she swallows and loses hold. At one point, she turns to Magnani and whispers, asks her, how do you say *I'm moved* in Italian, Magnani whispers a reply into Marilyn's hairdo, and then Marilyn leans into the microphone and says Comossa, sono comossa, e grazie, meeting them in their own language, and then they ask her what it means to receive this award, she must have received so many, why would this one be special, but Marilyn says the award *means a lot to me* and she hopes to prove herself deserving of it in the future. The microphones again, technical problems, and she says exactly the same thing one more time, in the same way, the award means a lot, she wants to be deserving of it in the future, it's what she's rehearsed, what she knows she's to say, and then the footage ends, 5:27 minutes of 1958 on YouTube.

Four years later Marilyn dies in bed in her Hollywood home, an overdose of barbiturates, an immortal Snow White or Sleeping Beauty, she implodes and drifts away into eternal sleep, whereas Anna Magnani, offended by something, slaps Brando's face, a misunderstanding, but still she slaps his face, once, twice, and Mamma Roma roars and weeps and howls as she runs back to the tenement, their home, runs from her market stall and all her vegetables, when she realises Ettore, her son, is lost to her, dead.

Marilyn, real *in a different reality*. If you don't expect anything good, what *do* you expect? If the reality is that reality is threatening? If by challenging someone's rage you put yourself at risk, you're not just going to slap that person in the face.

In Tana in the eighties I remember watching a programme hosted by Trond-Viggo Torgersen, *Nesten voksen* it was called, which translates as *Nearly Adult*. I remember the kids sitting in a circle on the floor around him, the way they so confidently spoke their minds, and I thought maybe Oslo could be an option for me too. The Cinemateket was in Oslo, showing the French New Wave, and to sit there and be sixteen, seventeen, and marvel at the way they could be like that, the French, with such assurance, the way they could say *No. Won't. Can't. Get away from me!* I couldn't do any of that. I didn't have it in me, that *No.* I was incapable.

'Liebster Jesu, wir sind hier', Matt tells her it's called, afterwards, when he's finished playing, the short hymn that seems almost to take Judith by the hands and lift her up, he stands at the row of benches where she's seated, *Liebster Jesu,* and drags his hair away from his face, she makes room and gestures for him to sit down, and Matt sits down, the cathedral is so silent, it's as if all the hymns are still there only they can't be heard, and he sits down beside her and looks at his hands, examines his fingers, they both look at his hands, as if the music were still contained in them, so that Jesus will remember us, says Matt, now that he's no longer here on earth, remember us and take us home with him.

And how many times has she heard Myrto at the piano, or conducting, in rehearsals, in concert, how many times has she tried to let the music enter her, to release inside her the way she saw it released inside him. But it just wasn't like that for her. He saw landscapes and occurrences, but she could see nothing and couldn't follow, her mind would build other structures instead, and the lines she saw in the external world repeated in her needlework, in ways no one else perhaps could see. She hadn't come to music in time. Only now, here, in the cathedral long afterwards, it unfolds for her, lays itself open, simple and clear.

11

If we hadn't held each other then, I perhaps wouldn't ever have seen him again. We were supposed to have been in Rome, I've no idea what I do the next day or the day after, I go to the gym in the morning, but then what? A beer with my lunch already, I don't know, all I know is my left knee hurts and I'm cold. At the same time, there's something that speaks *against* being afraid. The part of him that trembled seems truer to me than the angry half-adult who sat there shouting at me. It's that trembling I'm talking to, wordlessly, inside myself. It's when we're in *that* place together that I feel we belong with each other, that we're *us*. I check my notebook, but there's nothing from those few days, the pages are blank – what I do know is that I decide on the Wednesday to take that MDMA trip the Friday after, and I know that it's all to do with fear, that I want to get in behind it, and distance myself from it too, because it's a place I don't want to stay.

I've done it once before, taken MDMA, with a psychedelic therapist present. What happens is that the fear somehow gives way, mindscapes open up and you can *be* there in them without getting shut out. I do as I did with the therapist, I put some water by the bed, get the duvet plumped and ready. I've downloaded the playlist he sent me onto my iPad and now blend the crystals out of one of the shiny packets with a little water, drink, swallow, pour some more water into the glass, slosh it around and down it to make sure none goes to waste, and the taste is bitter and sharp. I put my sleep mask on, earbuds into my ears, lie back and wait. Some time passes and it doesn't feel like it's working, I'm unsure of the dosage, are M's scales exact enough, it didn't look like there was enough in that packet. Didn't he say too that a friend's girlfriend had done five hundred one time down in the south somewhere when she was on her own? After a while I get up and do another packet. I lie there, nothing happens, I do another. But still it's like it's not working. Eventually I do yet another packet. Now I've done four hundred milligrams and am lying there on my back with my sleep mask on and I feel like I'm going to be sick. I try and keep it in, but it's no use, I spew up, it runs down my cheeks, down my neck onto the pillow, onto my chest, everywhere, but something must have started working because I just lie there telling myself it's only water, I can clean it up later. For now, I'll let it all out, and deal with it later.

I record two voice memos on my phone, one at 16:52, another at 17:15. Before that I've been talking out loud to myself, I remember the sound of my voice, that it was comforting to hear myself out there somewhere, not just inside my head, but I can't remember what I said. It's when the trip's coming to an end that I pick up my phone and record these memos to myself.

Afterwards I sit in the kitchen and drink some water and at first I think: was that all, what was the point? The first trip I took was so radical, I experienced myself in such a completely new way, a sturdy, solid *self*, and all the men whose love I've ever received came to me one after another, I felt so much warmth, so much gratitude. But what sort of a trip was this, pukey and all on my own?

Just the one image, from inside his flat, *you really want to see me angry*? I was back there while I was tripping and suddenly I saw: M was a frightened little boy, a puny kid, afraid to death of the grown-up that was me, and in that image, the angry grown-up at the worktop in the kitchen throwing the pepper grinder at the wall (because I was afraid to death too), I saw his fear. I shouted out too, as I lay there under the duvet – *piccolo*, I shouted, *piccolo*, and I curled up and wept, because I heard the pain I saw in that image, I heard it in my voice, which was full of pain for him, that little boy, so afraid and alone he was.

From my notebook: "saw not myself, saw only M, how terrified he was – and it felt like *my* fear, *my* pain."

I've thought about it afterwards, wondered if seeing his pain so clearly, his rather than mine, the pain *I* felt in the kitchen at his place that night, was a let-down of sorts. But lying there in my bed and seeing how afraid he was, what I felt then was pity, a pity that went beyond just *you or me*, but pity all the same, which could be turned in any direction – and at bottom, pitying him was the same as pitying me.

Three days later I land back in Oslo and go straight from Gardermoen to see Pappa, he's thawed the prawns, cut the bread, set the table in front of the TV, put the butter, the mayo and the lemon out, and as soon as I come in through the door he takes my wine glass and shuffles into the kitchen to fill it up. We watch the news from Ukraine on the various channels, we see the bombed maternity clinic, the charred, gaping holes of the windows, as if those holes were the very bottom of the world.

I tell Pappa about M's anger and how afraid he made me feel, but it's like he doesn't hear how bad it was for *me.* He says, *You've got some ferocity in you, you should know.* As if he sees M's fear more than mine, *Mamma's afraid of you,* and we talk then about his own anger, he tells me about my younger brother when they had to wade over a stream once, it was after you stopped coming with me, he says and looks at me, because I stopped going with him up onto the fell, it's true, I was so afraid of your anger, I tell him, but he doesn't seem to be listening. He got soaked, but I put my foot in the wrong place and slipped and twisted my knee, it was agony and I turned on him, Pappa says with a shake of his head, it wasn't right of me, it wasn't right at all. And Mamma, I say, poor Mamma, because I saw that too when I was tripping the Friday before, I saw how afraid Mamma was, how afraid she'd been of Pappa all those years, I could really feel what that fear was, and she's never found another man since, never gone into any relationship with any other man after they split up and divorced when I was eighteen, after that there's been nothing, but still he's locked inside his own pain, Pappa, the little boy he was once, he's eighty-seven now and his eyes fill with tears, he pauses and looks at me – *Poor Mamma?* He shakes his head, sits there quietly a moment, then fixes his eyes on me, as if mystified and offended at the same time, and in a firm voice says: *Poor me, you mean.*

//

When I was there, I knew I was going to write something that would be set in Minneapolis, and when I returned to Milan and all those long days at the hospital with L, I would lie on the blue leatherette sofa next to his bed and read books I thought might be relevant, which could open up the landscape for me, that wide open landscape I thought I could feel my way into by virtue of my knowing something similar, the Finnmarksvidda, which are the plains of Finnmark, but the Finnmarksvidda is not the prairie, and the Sámi are not Native Americans, and I read so much, and kept on reading, but still I didn't know how to fit all this into the novel I wanted to write – would I have to go back there, rent a car, drive around and sleep at motels, maybe even in a tent out there in the wilderness?

I started with *Where the Dead Sit Talking*, a novel by a Native American writer I'd met in New York when we both were finalists at the National Book Awards, and after that I emailed him and asked where I should go from there, and he wrote back and told me to try Louise Erdrich. Her *Books and Islands in Ojibwe Country* is a meditation on a journey north with her eighteen-month-old daughter to the lakes and islands of southern Ontario, where the child's father, a Native American shaman or medicine man, lives. And in all Erdrich writes from this lakeland region, that other language, Ojibwe, resonates behind her English, the way Sámi resonated behind the Norwegian in Tana when I was growing up, a layer of something more, the water underlying the boggy plain, something more and other than, in everything, and the child's father, the medicine man, appears and they spend some time together before he sinks back into nature again, he paddles away in a canoe and disappears from sight behind an outcrop of land, and she's left alone with her little child, her daughter, and there's such a calm in everything, she and the child and the water, the sacred rock, the tobacco they offer up, and then just to rest there in the light of evening and simply exist.

And I've been wondering how I could write this into my novel, I know nothing about America, much less about Native American religions, nothing other than what I've been able to read, I've felt so helpless before that vast prairie into which, conceivably, I could venture, and wander endlessly without ever getting anywhere at all.

I recorded two voice memos, and the first is about the novel. Basically both are about the novel, only one has to do with M. Yes, both trips I took had the novel in them, but that doesn't mean I can just trip and the novel will be like *handed* to me, it means only that the novel *is me*, as I'm writing it, as it comes into being, that I too come into being with the novel, that the novel isn't something other than or external, it's a way of approaching and getting inside something I wouldn't otherwise know or see or be able to reach.

In the first voice memo, I say: *Il posto del amore è sempre sacro. Anche se è solo uno sguardo, è sempre sacro. Dove c'è amore, c'è sacro.* The place of love is always sacred. For me it was a message, a message *to* me, about getting here, inside the novel, because I'd been thinking so much about how I could write that sacredness into the novel – would I, for instance, make Matt Dillmann's mother a shaman? Would she then have encountered Myrto, seen Myrto, shared something with Myrto in such a way that she could then go to Judith and let Judith see, a kind of connection with him, now that Myrto was no longer there?

When I recorded the second voice memo half an hour later, my voice so very thin and translucent, as if shining through: Where is Myrto for Judith? Myrto is in the water, Myrto is in the air, Myrto is in the stars, Myrto is in everything, in nature, Myrto is in what is sacred, her love for Myrto is a holy place, love is sacred and he is in it all . . . Judith can only . . . sense it . . . sense that he's not just in one particular place, he's in all places.

I remind myself that I must ask my friend who lives there, a reader we met, my publisher and I, who I'm still in touch with, I must ask him about the stars in the sky above Minneapolis.

If we hadn't touched each other. But we did, we held each other and I felt M trembling, from a place where words don't exist, and where there is no meaning either, no explanation and no means of defence. Why couldn't I just let him go then? Let him go from inside me, I mean, let him go out the door, disappear into the street, turn the corner, and never, ever see him again?

//

What if it's fear I feel when he lets me hold him, without hiding himself, holding back, shielding. His fear. What if it's not the pulse of life I feel in him, but a fear so strong it can't be kept still?

Piccolo, I wanted to get inside that image and lift up that frightened boy and clutch him to my breast. To pick him up and never let him be alone with such fear again.

And gradually I see how alone he is, M, in all his days. Everything's so quiet around him, no one comes, there's no life in his house, the curtains are drawn, the dog sleeps in the corner under the table.

Long before this, in the winter, he takes a photo of me. Lake Como, we're there Saturday to Sunday, he's booked us a room at a small hotel, found an exhibition we can see, a walk we can take in the mountains. I take some photos of him too, at the top, he's sitting on a bench in the sun and I take a couple of him from inside the café, he's looking down at his phone and smoking, thinking. The one he takes of me, he's the only one who takes photos of me like that, who sees me like that, as if on some other level, uncovered, I've got my tongue sticking out of the corner of my mouth, unaware, as if I'm somewhere else inside myself, and although I'm looking at M as he takes the picture, it doesn't look like I know I'm visible to anyone.

As if he's seen something in me that can't actually be seen. Something no one else knows about. And there's another photo of me too, taken at a fairground, I'm there with my brothers and we're sitting on a merry-go-round, my younger brother slightly out of focus behind me, my older brother on a train engine of some sort, and then me in front on what looks like a boat or a ship, I'm holding on to a red-painted rudder, and I think it must be 17 May, Norway's independence day, because it looks like I'm wearing the finest *bunad*, the national dress, and in that photo too, which Pappa must have taken, because it was Pappa who took all the photos when we were little, I've got the exact same expression on my face, uncovered, or unknowing, my tongue in the same place, in the right-hand corner of my mouth.

Sounds come from further inside, someone in the kitchen, a tinkling of ice cubes in a glass, and it's not Judith, it's not Myrto either, it's Matt Dillmann, and now he comes back out, comes towards her, carrying a tray with two glasses on it, only he's not Clint Eastwood and she's not Meryl Streep, they're just Matt and Judith, and Matt has made iced tea, he's used the tall thin glasses she bought at a church bazaar when it was winter, but now it's not winter any more, a sudden, heavy warmth has descended on Minneapolis, and Matt puts the tray down on the table. He sits down beside her, as if this was a hundred and fifty years ago and she was the mother and he the son, or she was the aunt and he a younger relative, a younger brother, or just a neighbour, a friend, and they were pioneers in this vast and endless land and had at last found a moment in which to pause and take things in, to sit there a while beside each other, quietly, and see.

For how long can something be pleasant and unthreatening and yet *still* good? How long does it last? *I expected nothing good. Why did you have to go and DIE.* Why couldn't I just hold your hand and be at your side, be there with you, near to you, all night long, all the way through, until it was day again?

Are we put together from multiple parts, where some of those parts are rudimentary and primitive and small, while others are bigger, older, more grown-up, competent and responsible? Do all those parts rattle around in us, and who if anyone knows how they fit together? Is there someone who takes care of it all, who keeps us together, holds us tight and looks after us? Or is it all just parentless chaos in there, a legion of different-aged children, some retreated into the darkness of corners, others running around, boisterous and physical, sometimes at odds, while still others attempt to maintain order, meting out punishments and keeping the rest in check?

My tongue sticking out of the corner of my mouth, and there's the campfire outside the *gamme* and I'm ten years old and Pappa is the handsomest man in all the world, Mamma isn't with us, but the dog's there and my brothers are there, and Ruth and Jon, my cousins from Ørsta, Ruth four years older than me and so good at everything, the things women are supposed to be good at, cooking food and baking bread on the fire, thinking of others before themselves, and being soft and kind, and even though I'm good at those things too, pretty damn good in fact (though I wouldn't ever suggest as much to Pappa), even though I'm good at all that, Pappa never tells me so, instead he says, Look at Ruth, see how clever she is, how good she is, a proper *earth mother*, is what Pappa says, and it feels like he says this to me a number of times, and why did he do that, I wonder now, and as for *earth mother*, only me and my brothers knew what he meant by that, because it's everything Mamma wasn't, everything that was beyond her, but none of that's a problem for Ruth, she can manage it all, that's what Pappa says, with admiration and recognition in his voice, deep in all his ruddiness, and he can't help but see, I think to myself now, he must have seen how sad it made me, and he couldn't say anything nice to my brothers either, though he could speak well about them to others, me for example, when they weren't listening, he could brag about how good at fishing Jon was, and what kind of crap was that, I think to myself now, what kind of a fucking way was that to treat your own children.

They sit there, each with a glass of iced tea.

It's so vast.

In Judith's eyes it widens, that glittering place underneath the water. Matt looks over the top of his glass as they sip their tea. He hides his smile. She too. And they begin to laugh.

And this is how it will be from now on, Matt coming to the green house on 297 Dayton in the evenings from time to time. Judith cooks dinner for them, they eat at the wooden table in the kitchen or sitting on the floor in the living room with their plates on the sofa, Matt watches TV or does homework or practises on the piano, at night his young body lies heavily on the bed and Judith looks at it in wonderment, and in the morning he lies with his eyes closed and pulls up his T-shirt, invites her with a movement of his hand to caress him, and her hand moves softly and quietly, over his chest, his belly, his arms, and it's as if he was a small bird ascending from a well a thousand feet deep, and when at last he peeps over the top his cock is hard and ready, she kisses it softly before cautiously getting on top of him, as if allowing him to ascend that last little bit of the way, into the daylight, into her heart.

//

I've started dropping in on Pappa whenever I'm back in Oslo, just to sit with him for a bit in the evenings, I never used to, and he'll have the TV on and sometimes we'll talk, but mostly we just sit there. Now Pappa's made himself a G&T and after he's sat down on the sofa again he lifts his glass to me and asks me if I think there's reason to toast, I don't know what he means, Finland and Sweden joining NATO, he says, but you're my political adviser, I joke, if you're in favour we'll toast, and so we do, and there aren't as many images from Ukraine that night, but a lot from Stockholm, Pappa's been following the parliamentary debate there live all day and the evening news has the prime minister and the leader of the opposition shoulder to shoulder announcing that they're fully behind the country's NATO application.

I tell him I've been wondering about the hitting and can I ask him about it, and he says yes, and I ask him then about the feeling he says he has, the feeling of being no one, nothing, and whether he thinks it has anything to do with Farmor hitting him when he was growing up. No, Pappa says, he thinks it's to do with something else that predates it, he was maybe three months old when they set off home from China in the autumn of 1935, it was four months on board the ship, he says, and there were six older siblings to be looked after. They always said, later, his siblings, that no one cared about him, he says, it was as if I didn't really count, and perhaps I didn't even then, he says, on the ship. But what about being hit, I ask him, what did that do to you, and Pappa says then that it made sense enough, as a system. It was a punishment, Pappa says, I'd do something wrong and be punished for it. Mother was fair, he says, and tells me about a time one summer, it was hot and they were haymaking, mowing the hay and hanging it to dry on the racks, and everyone had to do their bit, only he'd made himself scarce and gone down to the Vik river to do some fishing instead, he came home with a whole stringful of fish, dinner for the entire family, he says with a laugh, but no matter, he was still marched into the barn and beaten for not having played his part, because there were rules, he says, and the rules for hanging the hay to dry said that everyone had to take part whether they wanted to or not, and that included him.

Really want to see me angry. Why am I seeing him again after that? The MDMA showed me a frightened little boy. But why can't I just leave it at that? What can I do about it anyway?

On the Friday, in the kitchen after that MDMA trip, the glass I drank from held in my hand, I'm voice-messaging M on WhatsApp. Because in one of those memos I recorded, the one that was about him and not the novel, I say I love him, we can't be together, but maybe I can help him. I message him and tell him about how afraid I was when I was little and that I'd like to be there for him, together with him, if he wants to confront his fear. Seven messages I send him, twenty minutes at least in all, but then my friend calls, the one who needed crisis support that time, and when I tell him about the messages I've sent he says, Don't, don't even think about going there. That makes me afraid again and so I delete them all before M's had time to listen to them.

But still it won't go away. Maybe M could do an MDMA trip himself? I could be there with him, to support him.

Back in Milan, the weather's so hot. Milanese spring is like full-on summer back home, time doesn't connect between here and there. Inside me too, it's like I'm somewhere in between, out of breath, I feel an urgency, I can barely get my shoes on properly before I'm out the door.

He sends me things, though not often, and not words or thoughts, but pictures, and I think of them as signs, signals across the water, a day or two might pass, he sees someone in the street with a funny walk and sends me a video of them to make me laugh, or a photo of light striking a lamp post, the shadow cast behind it, and he doesn't apologise, Pappa didn't either when we were kids, not a single time, as if once it's happened it's gone. Still, after a while I text him and ask him if he wants to do an MDMA trip like the one I did with my therapist, only with me at his side. A few hours go by before he replies: Yes.

We agree he can come over to mine the following Saturday. I wake up in the night, what if he comes through the door and hits me. Less afraid during the day, then afraid when night comes again. What have I started. I can always cancel, I tell myself, only I don't.

What am I hoping for? A miracle? That something will open up inside him, really open up, and be met, be seen and embraced, changed, transformed? Wouldn't that be a miracle? That the good in him came out stronger than his hardness and anger, that his vulnerable side and all his verve won out and described him completely, and that this took place on a Saturday morning on my sofa with the aid of MDMA?

Judith and Matt with their tall glasses in the heat on the porch on 297 Dayton Avenue. Aren't you supposed to be at school now, Judith is about to ask, but what kind of a thing is that to say. Enquist, in *The Parable Book*, writes of his encounter with *the woman on the knot-free pine floor*. He's now seventy-seven years old and has never written about it before, this encounter that for him was to become so transformative and which took him *right inside the meaning of life, at the very centre, deep down, into the meaning of everything, and this was what the meaning of life was, more wondrous than redemption*. He's fifteen at the time and lies reading in the grass, a Sunday in July in the far north of Sweden, in the hot sun, and he's invited in for lemonade by a Stockholmer who's rented a cottage there for the summer, she's much older than him, fifty-one, and she invites him into the kitchen, and there she lets him come inside her, on the floor. This happens quite simply, with no other build-up than her suggesting to him that she's a medical assistant and that she wishes to examine whether he has any difficulty pulling back his foreskin. She smiles obliquely, it says, closes both her eyes, and her *fingertips flutter and skip over his penis*, he enters her a fraction, perhaps two centimetres at first, and then: *right inside the meaning of life, at the very centre*, and it's all so quiet and cautious and almost *divine*, Enquist writes. They'd never meet again after that, and she: *Never tell anyone*, and he promises. This is Enquist's encounter with love, something opens up in him and he is changed for good. He'd never written about it, not until then.

The encounter with love as a miracle. What if the miraculous encounter is possible? An encounter with love, with the very core of one's being? It sounds simple, naive perhaps. But what if it really *is* simple, deep down?

And the two of them sitting there in the shade on the porch, with iced tea, and Judith looks at Matt as he gazes at the yellowed grass, she sees his hair slanted down across his nose, his fair eyelashes, and he turns his head towards her and they look at each other and she tries to recall the way Myrto would look at her, the feeling of being good enough. Nothing in his eyes ever pushed her aside. *So there you are.* As if every time he looked at her was a moment of happiness at his eyes seeing her again: So good that you came.

The helmet makes his head look far too big on top of his slender frame, he's like some leggy insect, his glasses, a strident ant, M manoeuvres his heavy e-scooter out of the lift and into the hall. It's gone half past twelve, we'd said twelve, and now he's hungry, he's hungry because he knows he won't be able to eat, and he wants to eat, he wants to sabotage what we've agreed, there's a part of him that wants to back down and go back out the door. That's what I think. And I'm sort of afraid underneath, inside, there's a shadow over his eyes, as if he's afraid too, but I get the earbuds ready and the sleep mask, I mix the crystals, he drinks and washes it down, just the one dose, he doesn't want more than that, and then lies back on the sofa. I'm just there in the living room with him, going about, normally I'd have wanted to get some work done, some writing, but now he's lying there on the sofa and I really hope something good's going to happen, something good for him, that he's going to sense the light I see in his eyes, the times he's allowed it to shine on me, and sense that the light is his, that it's him.

But will it be him if he doesn't want that, if he won't choose it, if he won't seek it out and waken it, cultivate it, hold it carefully in both hands and clutch it gently to his chest – will it still be him then?

At the same time: how can you choose something if you don't know it's there? If he doesn't know that he is that light, and not (as he'll later say) a dark, defiant will that his father had to beat down to make him a person whose presence in the world the rest of us could live with.

I record him as he starts to speak, the sleep mask still covers his eyes. His voice is completely soft, as if from the depths of his throat, from deep down inside him, and what he says is: You will stay with me for always, always, you will stay with me. He sounds like he means it. It makes me so happy. He says that I'm Bella, Buona and Brava, three B's, he says, and smiles, pleased with himself for putting it that way, You're my 3B, he says and he says I'm intelligent too. I record him for twenty minutes before switching it off. After a while he starts sweating, he doesn't want the sleep mask on any more, takes a cigarette break on the balcony before lying down again, and he wants me close to him then, I'm so tense that I've opened a beer and poured myself a glass, I put it under the sofa and sit down on the floor next to him and hope he won't notice, the beer, and then I just sit there.

For several hours I sit, he holds my hand and his other hand is like a big mitt he lifts and then lowers to stroke the back of my own, very softly, with the tips of his fingers, lifting and lowering, it could have been to scratch, to claw, but that's not what he does, he's gentle, his hand passing over mine, again and again, and it's all so very timid, so very soft, and he doesn't hurt me.

//

Does anything change after that MDMA trip? He thanks me for the nicest afternoon he's had in ages. But is he more loving, less aggressive?

I call him a few days later, normally he's the one who phones, I text or DM, but now I pick up the phone and call him, it's the middle of the day and light as I walk along the busy street that runs past my building, I've something to do in town, I tell him I've got it into my head that he's bought himself a Defender and that it's red, and I ask him if it's true, if he's told me about it or if it's just something I dreamed. He goes quiet, then answers me in a way that sounds like yes, only not quite, and I don't understand, but I can tell he's pleased about something.

He's been dying to own a car like that ever since we went hiking in the mountains near France shortly after we first met, I don't know how many hundreds of metres we ascended, the trail, a piste in winter, went straight up into the air, but M was soon so exhausted he could only take the smallest of steps, while I marched on, the last bit of the way was so steep I didn't dare turn and look back over my shoulder, and I didn't want to think about what could happen if I lost my footing, I was only wearing the worn-out Adidas trainers L had given me a few years before, and when at last we got to the top, relieved and trembling, we wandered about for a bit, there's a crumbling old fortress up there with several buildings, and there, parked between the stone walls, were several Defenders, and some of them had roof tents, and that was when it started, it was on that walk in the mountains that he said one day we were going to have a car like that with a roof tent so we could just drive off anywhere, and immediately I thought: *As far away as we can. We'll look out through the windows, at fells and towns and lakes, and talk to people from foreign lands. We'll be together all the time. And forever be on our way.*

On our way up over the first hump we went over to the edge and lay down under some big trees. Flat out on my back, and I remember the wind rustling the leaves high above. M turned his head and looked at me, his brown eyes flecked with sky. I didn't know what was in them. But if it was real, what I could see, what I could glimpse, if what would suddenly appear in his eyes, gleaming out at me, if that was real, a warmth so dark and big, so soft and tender, if that place inside him really existed and could open out and be ours, if we could go there, the two of us, and be there together, then yes, in that case it was the only thing I wanted, ever.

A week later he's actually gone and done it. Bought a bright red Defender. He'd been looking at it online before I phoned him. He asks if I want to come with him when he goes to pick it up. And me, I'm right there with my chirpy *yes*, and he says then that we'll have to get the train, that there's one after lunch, so I'll be able to make the gym in the morning, then I can go over to his afterwards and we can take the Metro together to Centrale, and get the train from there. Yes! I chirp. And even though I'm afraid, I check the train times and find a departure that costs half of what M's suggesting and which only takes twenty minutes longer, and I ask him if that's okay, to buy those tickets instead, but I'm still not really looking forward to it when I pack my bag on the Tuesday morning, I'm taking my Mac so I can write on the train, it's a long journey, to Savona and then north from there.

I secure my bike to the fence in his yard, take off my helmet and go towards his entrance door, there are paths with grass in between leading to the different stairways, it's like the way up to a big house in the country, and there's already a warmth in the air, the sun's come up. I key in the code and go up the stairs, M lives at the top, in the corner, and I'm not sure what to expect. I knock, then pull the handle down, the door's open, the dog comes out from under the table and wags not only her tail but her entire *tail end*, and I crouch down, pat and scratch her, hear the water in the pipes, M's in the shower upstairs, I dump my bag, my bike helmet, take off my shoes and go up the stairs, calling out a *hello* so as not to give him a fright, the bathroom door's open, all these open doors, Pappa was the same, always leaving the door open, even on the loo, and I see him from the top of the stairs, I can see over the top of the bed into the bathroom, I can see him standing there naked in the shower in the corner and he's so beautiful, and then he sees me, he looks straight at me, and smiles.

He hobbles down the stairs, he twisted his ankle at work the day before, he hadn't told me, he can hardly walk, but he's not complaining, I ask him if he'll be able to drive when we get there, it's a long way back, several hours, but he says it won't be a problem, he says he's glad they brought him up the way they did, his parents, when he was a kid and fell down it was always, Up you get, no whinging, no hysterics. His ankle's really swollen.

On the way to the Metro he can barely put his foot down, he asks how much I think a taxi would cost to Centrale, maybe twenty euros, I say, and he hobbles on, there's a chemist's a bit further along, he wants to go in and get an ice pack then grab a taxi from there, and that's when I realise how bad it is and I'm sorry for not having insisted on a taxi from home, I tell him so, I know how much you like to walk, he says, but I can walk any time, that's not important now, he's hobbled all this way for my sake, and I think about my daughter and the time she had stomach pains, some kind of poisoning due to cross-medication, and they sent us from our GP straight to Ullevål and I didn't listen then either, when the doctor told us to get a taxi, we took a number 20 bus and I've always been sorry about it, she was all right, so it's not that, it was me not showing her any understanding, not showing her that she was important, her being in pain, and now I've gone and done it again, not listened.

Susan Sontag, *Regarding the Pain of Others.* I bought it on Amazon last year and still haven't read it. I also got hold of the book her son wrote when she died of cancer, eventually died of cancer, because she'd had it several times, and she wouldn't talk about death either, the same as L. *Swimming in a Sea of Death*, it's called. And I think about Sally Mann's photo assignment for *National Geographic*, her series from the so-called *body farm* belonging to the University of Tennessee, a fenced-in area where dead bodies are left out in the elements so that every conceivable aspect of death and putrefaction can be studied scientifically. *What Remains*, she called the series, and there's a quiet dignity in those photographs, so delicate the bodies are, flecked and decomposing, *and you should see the colours*, Mann says, *they're really beautiful.* In the same interview she says she's doing a series about her husband, Larry, he's been a model of hers more than forty years, *Larry has such confidence in my art*, she says, *far more than I have*, and now he's suffering from muscular dystrophy, and she's documenting that, a series of near-abstract images of lines and shadows and skin, but this is something else, she says, this is a much bigger series she's been doing almost forever, she says, *still in love, still at work*, Larry in different situations, domestic, paternal, sexual. It's a series yet to be revealed, *Marital Trust*, she calls it.

The platform our train's leaving from is the one that's furthest away of them all, and M hobbles and hops and I tell him I can carry him if only I can get him onto my back, and I mean it, and know I could have done too, but M's too proud, or too bashful, he just smiles at me, and I don't know what that smile means, whether he's with me or against, whether he's bearing up and feels he has to be alone with his pain, or is thankful.

The train's a double-decker. He manages to get up the stairs, preferring to sit on the top deck, but the air conditioning's broken in the first coach, it's too hot without it, so we go back downstairs, then up again in the next. We roll out of the station, soon it's open fields we see, houses and farms here and there, trees and hills. I've got my Mac open on my lap, M's on the seat facing me, he's reading on his phone. After an hour or so I film him, ten seconds, he's looking down, but then he must have sensed something, he looks up, and I've zoomed in by then, he looks straight at the camera, or at me, and after a moment it's as if he surrenders, that's what I'd have wanted to write, only he doesn't, there's something in him that's holding back, but something else too that opens out, in his face, and gleams in his eyes, and he smiles.

In Alessandria we have to change trains and there's a forty-minute wait, we buy focaccia from the station's café, and four small beers, there aren't any of the bigger ones, they put it all in a paper bag for us and we go back to the platform where M wants to smoke a joint, he hobbles off down the platform to stand away from the other passengers while he smokes, and we stand there together in the sunshine, I take a couple of drags and M smokes the rest. When we get on the train he opens another ice pack to put against his ankle. There's a tenderness between us that I haven't known for some time. And as we sit there quietly together just looking at each other every now and then, I feel myself wanting him. A short while ago he said, casually, as if by the way, as he often does when there's something he's actually been thinking about quite a lot, Do you want to as well, and what he meant was sex, and the thought was planted in me then, and has lingered.

Do you want to as well, and I wonder about it myself, have always wondered about it, ever since I first got married a long time ago, when I was younger than my daughter is now, because it's what he said too, *Do you want to as well*, and I didn't, not really. Not the way everyone else does apparently, the way it looks in the media, in newspapers and magazines, all pert little tits and bums, a bulge in the trousers, or the way they walk, the men, their muscular thighs, their long male legs, their strong arms and shoulders, the look in their eyes. I've wished I was in on all that, only I'm not. But sitting there on the train I want it anyway, and in that realisation I understand something about myself. I understand that for me sexual desire hasn't got anything to do with body shape or a person's way of moving, it's not like M's relaxed at the hip and holds his shoulders straight and his head high, and it's not his hands either, which are rough and calloused, or that I so much like the lines of his face, which look like someone drew them in charcoal, no, he could have looked completely different and it would have been the same, because what made me want him close up against me, what made me want to feel him and be naked with him, was *him*, was *this*, this tenderness, the way it opened out for us again, in all its softness, and at that exact moment everything felt safe. And when we have sex with each other, when we go into all that's good about us, when we open ourselves to each other, then there's no one else I've ever been so close to, no one who's let go of their body against mine the way he does. Sex with M when we're in that place together is making love, his entire strong, slender body is laid open in mine, and every time he comes inside me it's as he says, again and again, the greatest, most beautiful, most important thing there is, that I'm his and he's mine, and *here is where I want to be.* I understood that exactly *this* was the nature of my desire, as I sat there opposite him that day on the train.

//

Have I always been afraid? Was fear transferred to me when I was in the womb and Pappa out with his axe? Mamma was always afraid. And me? From before there was any language in which to even say the word, was there nothing there to hold on to? I don't know. And does that mean it's my own fear that's the problem, rather than M's aggression? If I had less fear inside me, would things be better for us?

As a person she was sensitive and there was something vulnerable about her . . . Knaus describing you in Book Six, a friend texts. It makes me think about the therapist I was seeing that time after my divorce when I was reading Alice Miller and thought I had to go into therapy with a male therapist in order to learn how to love, he shoved a big pillow into my lap and told me I needed to learn how to protect myself. I didn't go back to him.

Together with two girlfriends I go off to the preview of the Biennale, one of them is my curator friend, the one with the risotto, the three of us have got a suite with silk wallpaper and a wonky floor and I share the four-poster with her, the curator, I'm afraid even though M's a long way away, everything hurts the whole time and I don't know why, I can't sleep at night, I toss and turn, the whole bed bouncing, my fear a mesh beneath my skin.

Unprotected is another way of saying open, and I've always thought of it as a strength, I've connected it with my writing, to be open-chested and present a broad front. My girlfriend wangles us into a private party for Marlene Dumas. I'm not that bothered about meeting and greeting, I think about how many people Marlene Dumas must meet all the time, even just there, that night, for me it's her work that's important and I can see that anytime, but towards the end I meet her up close anyway, my girlfriend introduces me and Marlene smiles and squeezes my hand, nods warmly and kindly when I try to say something about what her work means to me and that I've even written about it and *blah blah blah*, and I tell her this while smiling the whole time, and she *blah blah blahs* too and performs a flourish, we laugh, and then she's ushered over to someone else. But it wasn't that. What made an impression on me was *seeing* Dumas. Her small frame, how soft she appeared. The way she turned to the person she was talking to and yet seemed almost to be facing the person behind her too. As if her body was too soft by far. As if everything inside her, to the very edges of her, was open.

She's far too amenable, my curator girlfriend says afterwards. She's got two assistants, a man and a woman, who shield her, if they hadn't been there it wouldn't have been possible. They look after her, she's way too accessible. Two full-time assistants to give her protection, I think to myself. And who's looking after me?

I take pictures of M beside the Defender. The young man who's selling it has picked us up at the station and driven us along a narrow winding road up through the forest. They fetch the original rear door and a window from the barn, M hobbling, but I'm not allowed to help, they load them inside. He's given the keys and hands me one set straight away – these are yours, he says.

The engine's noisy and we're not going very fast, occasionally touching a hundred, we don't talk much, but I can tell he's pleased, and when we stop to fill up for the first time I almost have to fight him before he'll let me pay.

It's as if he darkens as we near Milan, and outside it darkens too, we're hungry, we're going to celebrate, of course, but right now we just need to find somewhere to eat before they close, and I say anything's all right for me apart from the Autogrill, how about Rathouse, he asks, and I understand it's where he went with his aunt and his parents not so long ago when it was his aunt's birthday, fine by me, I say with a smile. He parks the Defender next to another 4x4 that looks small and puny in comparison, Imagine what the driver'll think when he comes back out and sees this, M says. But "Rathouse", as he pronounces it, isn't Rathouse, it's Roadhouse, another sort of Autogrill, only a different chain, and I don't know what to make of it, it's just such a dreary place inside, I don't know what to choose from the menu, and I'd like to have some wine, but when I get back from the loo M's ordered beer for us, and all the time we're there it's as if his father's there too, as if going there to eat after buying the Defender is M's way of connecting with him again, because it was supposed to have been the two of them who went to collect the car, his father was meant to be co-owner, the insurance would have been cheaper then, but his father changed his mind and was against the whole purchase, so M ended up on his own with it, and that was when he asked me.

Two beers each, and something's about to tip, but we keep our balance, we go out to the car and it's not far to his place, he parks inside the fence and locks the gate, and hobbles towards the door. He rides the lift up, I use the stairs, and then I take the dog out because M really can't walk with that ankle of his, I pick up the lead, she fusses with excitement and bundles out through the door, and while we're out on the adjoining waste ground I phone Camilla, I haven't answered her all day, I told her I had to go somewhere with a friend, but not that the friend was M, because she thinks it's over for good between us and is glad about it, because I've told her how afraid I've been, and every time the dog runs too far off all I have to do is call her name, not even that loudly, or give a short whistle, and she comes straight back.

Inside again, M's sitting on the sofa smoking, the balcony door's ajar, I take a couple of drags too, and then it's as if everything lets go inside me, in my chest, my stomach, and we have sex with each other and I come several times, and only he can make me come like that, *bella*, he says softly, while gazing at me.

That night we sleep close together. When I wake up in the darkness and discover he's turned away onto his side and I reach my hand out, he takes it in his sleep, and holds tight.

//

I've only got two nights, Wednesday and Thursday, before I go back to Oslo, and at first M says he's busy Wednesday, but we can see each other Thursday, on the Wednesday he's got to sort something out at his storage facility, he and a friend of his, and I'm relieved because it's seldom a good idea for us to see each other two days in a row, it's as if somehow our relationship can't contain it, I don't know, but then on the Wednesday he phones and says his friend can't come until the day after, so he can see me the same night if I want – does he feel obliged with me going away for some time? I've told him before that it's much better not to see each other if he's not in the mood for it, because I can feel it then and it makes me nervous, and there must be a part of me too that isn't sure, because when he texts me around seven I type back that I'm watching *The Fugitive Kind* again and want to see it to the end – am I trying to tell him I'm not some drooling little dog waiting for him to give the word? Around eight the film's finished and I phone him and ask if he wants me to come round. *Mi farebbe piacere*, he says, and I think I react to that immediately, there's a lack of enthusiasm about the phrase, *that'd be nice*, he said the same thing earlier on too, like I was his aunt and not his girlfriend, but still I pack my bag, again I pack my bag, we'll rustle up something quick to eat at home, and so I take with me some things from the fridge, a puntarelle salad, anchovies and garlic for the dressing, a couple of beers and the bottle of white wine we opened together the week before. I know it's pushing it with regard to the drink, so when I get to his I try and sneak the wine into the fridge without him noticing.

There's something about him when I get there, I don't know what it is, but it makes me feel unsettled. It's hot, we're sitting out on the balcony at the table he's only just bought, I sent him some pictures one morning of outdoor furniture for sale on Marketplace and when I came round the same evening he'd been to a second-hand shop nearby, a place his mother knew about, and bought this old table made of iron and two benches, and so that's where we're sitting, he's quiet and withdrawn, any talk is down to me, I tell him what I'm going to be doing in Oslo, all the appointments I've got from early to late in the day, but he just sips his beer in silence, he doesn't even look at me, then he interrupts and comments on something in the street, though without following up, so I have to carry on myself, and what am I doing there, why did he ask me round, it doesn't feel like he wants me there at all.

Why don't I just leave then? Why do I go with him to the pizzeria, with the dog too, he shoves her underneath the table with his foot, we take a large beer each from the fridge and I drink all of mine, but he doesn't drink half of his, he shoves it away across the table and fetches himself a Coke instead. It's a quarter to twelve when I decide to go to bed, but don't go to sleep, he says, I'll be up in a minute for some *coccole*, which means a cuddle, and so I lie there trying to stay awake, because I want to cuddle him too, but he's taking such a long time and when it gets to a quarter past I decide I'll go downstairs and tell him I'm going to sleep, only he's not in the living room and not on the balcony either. I can hear noises through the door next to the kitchen that leads out to where the bathroom is, I realise that's where he is, and I can hear he's watching something, a video of some sort, and I wonder what he's watching, porn, I guess, sex and violence, and I knock at first, but then I open the door very suddenly, because I want to see what he's doing, and there he is sitting completely naked on the toilet, and he's startled, and raises his arm as if to protect himself, and says, *Scusa, scusa*, in a little child's voice. I don't understand what's happening, there's nothing to apologise for, I say quietly, I was just wondering where he was, you said you wanted coccole, only I can't keep myself awake any longer, I tell him, and with that it's as if he shifts into some other place inside himself and abruptly, in a hard voice now, he says, with a wave of his hand, that I can just go to bed, he'll be up in a minute, and I can tell he just wants me out of there, and so I go away and close the door behind me and go back upstairs and get into bed, turn the light out, and I can't remember any more after that.

I can't remember any more until I wake up at four o'clock, and I've been awake before that as well, but every time I've reached a hand out to him, he's pulled away. What do I do now, what I really want is to cycle home, but I know that if I cycle home now it'll be the end of everything; still, I'm so on edge, and I remember the wine in the fridge, so I tiptoe down the stairs and sit with a glass, only it doesn't help, so I have another, and it's only after I've drunk the lot that I can feel a certain effect, and I go back up the stairs and climb back into bed and fall asleep.

It wasn't a good move. I think something in me knew that already when I put the bottle in my bag before coming out. He's furious. It's half past six in the morning and when I try and explain to him that I was so on edge and that he was pushing me away from him, all he says is that I reek of alcohol and *You know I can't stand it.* But that only came afterwards, I explain, I was so on edge, I had myself a drink in order to sleep, not because I wanted to go, I tell him, because I wanted to stay, but he's not listening, he's furious, he hasn't had enough sleep and he keeps repeating, over and over, what a despicable thing I've done, ranting, winding himself up, until he's completely beside himself, like he's freaking out on something. And again I put on my bike helmet, I take the salad from the fridge and wriggle into my backpack, walk out the door and down the stairs, but then when I get to my bike I stop and turn round and go back up, because if I go now I won't see him for weeks and I don't want us to part like this, Won't you hold me, I say in the hall with my helmet still on, and he just says, *Not when you stink like that*, and I look up at him and start crying and sink down onto my haunches, and he says he hates it when I cry, and so I just leave, I go back down to my bike and unlock it and very cautiously I cycle home along the road in the light of morning.

It's the evening before I leave now, I've been to the gym and packed my things and cried, Now it's too much of a problem, he texts, thanks for everything. It seems like to his mind it's all about the alcohol, if it wasn't for that everything would be all right between us, and of the two of us it's me who drinks.

But for me it's more complicated, there's so much I don't understand, there are swathes of him that are light and tender and where everything trembles, but then there's the other side of him, his darkness and everything he's not telling me, and when I come home from the gym that day I bump into his father, he's on his way out with M's aunt and I hold the door for them, we say hello and I force a smile, but as soon as I see the father's eyes I feel a sudden tension in my groin and I know what that is, it's *fear*, and he doesn't smile back, his eyes are like fish scales, a dense interlocking barrier that feels like contempt. And when later I'm sitting in the kitchen on my own, it's just gone ten o'clock, a couple of glasses and I'll be on my way to bed, I can't help myself, I text M and ask how old he was when his father started hitting him. He texts back and says he exaggerated, it wasn't that bad, his father probably ought to have punished him more than he did. I feel quite despairing, I type *nervo di bue* into Google's search bar, M told me that was what he hit him with, and it's a flogging instrument made from the sinews of an ox, from a bull's penis, for instance, that's what it says, and I look at various images, they're quite short and plaited, and used on beasts of burden, it says, or on humans, as an instrument of torture. My hands are trembling, what did he do to M, my own beautiful boy, and I type back and say, *Next time I see your father I'll ask him: Did it give you a kick, using your whip on M?* and I mute my phone then and go to bed.

I wake up at 5:20 and the first thing I see is that the whole screen's full, he's been texting, phoning, all night long, he can't have gone to sleep. The same all the way through, DON'T YOU DARE MENTION MY FAMILY, and I'm an alcoholic and a completely useless writer and he's going to destroy me bit by bit, and I'm NEVER to even THINK ABOUT approaching his aunt or his parents ever again. As if I ever have. I'm shaking now, and write back before even thinking, *I won't say anything to your father, I promise.* It's the first thing that comes into my head, and all I want is to calm him down, but he comes right back at me: I don't believe you, you're the last person in the world I'd trust. He's got some very sick thoughts, he writes, about what he's going to do to me, and it goes on like this, non-stop, until half past eight when eventually I block his number. I undo it again a bit later, but he's stopped texting by then, there's nothing more.

I go to the gym and do a quick session before catching the airport shuttle and it's on the mat on the floor in the gym that I sense I'm afraid in a different way now than before.

It's what Camilla said to me the last time I cycled home from his at night and texted her to ask if we could talk, because she's savvy and she knows M, we sat on a bench by the canal and she was unequivocal: This time it's just words, but what about next time? Her eyes said to me: Is that where you want to go? Do you really want to go there? Even someone who raises his voice, Camilla said, even a raised voice is enough for me to say Ciao, and she made a gesture with her hand like when you shove a cat out of the way, ciao. Ciao. I picture my front door up on the sixth floor, in the corner, and my half-deaf neighbour on the other side of the landing, he's more than ninety years old, and I wonder if M will be standing there when I get back from the gym, because he's got a key to the door in the rear courtyard, whether he'll be standing there waiting to do to me what he's been texting all night, and what will I do then, I'm too afraid to go home, I text Camilla and ask if she'll go with me, but she doesn't see it, she must still be asleep, she's heavily pregnant, and then I remember the concierge, I can ask him to go to my door with me, and that's what I do, I ask him as soon as I come in through the entrance downstairs, and he's so good about it, I feel I'm about to start crying, I'm so afraid, I tell him, is it someone from the building, he wants to know, but I've been in Italy long enough not to be as open about such things as I would have been before, so I tell him it's someone out there, and I nod vaguely in the direction of the city, and he says Milan's a dangerous place, you've got to be careful, and once we've gone up in the lift and I'm letting myself in, I ask him if he can add his name and number into my contacts so

I can let him know when I'm ready to come down again with my suitcase, and he takes my phone and types, and I didn't even know his name, but when I look at the display I see the irony, he's called Sherif.

11

Unfinished, Schubert's Symphony No. 8, was what Myrto had been so looking forward to working with in Minneapolis. Judith puts it on in the living room and turns the volume up high so they can listen to it together outside, she and Matt. It begins so cautiously, like a person walking very quietly through the grass of a wide meadow, lifting their legs, and then the hum of the flute, like someone else walking just as quietly, thoughtlessly, at your side, and from the meadow the two of you enter the woods, and though the sun is shining it's not hot, it's nice and warm, the light descends through the leaves, and the melody makes you stride now, there's both rest and hope in everything. But that's just the beginning. After that it complicates. And after a while she falls by the wayside, even though she wants to stay with it, even though she's resolved, but further in than this the sounds no longer make sense to her. Myrto, she thinks, this unrestful turmoil, he was here too, in this, but to her the sounds grow and entangle, and the woods are no longer simple but bewitched. Louder now, the music rises like a wall in front of her. Myrto! She doesn't know what to do, remains standing at the mirror in the hallway where the stairs lead up, Matt outside, the rooms of the house behind her. A turmoil, she too. Perhaps that's just the way it has to be, she thinks after a moment. Perhaps *Unfinished* took Myrto away into some woods inside himself somewhere, a place unknown to her. Woods that she'll never know anything about.

But what if there wasn't a system, I ask Pappa. We're quiet as Ukraine's president looks straight into the camera and says, *We will not give up*, the chunky tanks tipping and rolling like toys in a children's sandpit, but this is no game, we exchange glances and *we'll stay here all through winter*, his rucksack there in front of me as we cross through the heather. And Farmor, at the back of the barn, *Mother was fair*, Pappa said the last time I was here, but what if you were just being beaten at will, I say, what does that do to you, and Pappa says, Then you're like this, and he demonstrates, waving his arms in self-defence. I look at Pappa and then I turn my head away because suddenly I realise, I see it as clear as day, when I went downstairs and found M sitting there on the toilet like that, the way he jumped and cowered, the way he raised his arm, *scusa*, that little child's voice, and of course I don't know for sure, but suddenly it's like everything sinks back as if to allow an overview, and I think it wasn't the way I maybe thought, that his mother was a drinker and unable to protect him from his father, because he told me not long ago that she doesn't drink, a single glass makes her dizzy, now I'm thinking he was the one who drank, the father, he drank, and when he was drunk and out of his senses he'd come bursting into where M was and take off his belt, or grab the whip or whatever it was, and then set about offloading everything he just couldn't manage to carry around. And that's why, when I drink, M is so angry, and underneath that so afraid, even after one beer there may be something inside him that starts to cower, and when *I've* had too much I become the father, the two of us blur together, the father and me, and his fear then becomes so complete that there's no longer any difference, between me and his father, because more than anything else drunk to him means danger.

I can't be sure that's how it is, and I can't ask him either.

The father's version, that's become his own: M needed bringing into line, otherwise things would have gone wrong for him, because M was a tearaway, he was out of control, and his father was only doing it because he wanted to help him, to put him on the straight and narrow, it was for his own good, he was doing it out of love.

And then he meets me and I'm seventeen years older and something in him believes I can help him, that I can bend down and pick him up and take him with me, *piccolo*, we can drive away in the Defender, but I can't manage that, I can't, because his fear feeds straight into mine and makes me afraid, me too, together with him I become the frightened little girl I used to be, and she too needs to be looked after, but then all we are is just two frightened kids and there's no one there to help.

I tell Pappa what I texted to M, *Next time I see your father I'm going to . . .* that I just wanted to show that I'm on M's side and bring him round to that too. But Pappa shakes his head. No, no, he almost blurts, ugh, no. It's no wonder he was angry, Pappa says, and looks at me, and his eyes are as if streaked with the darkest pain. He's bound up in having been beaten, Pappa says, he needs you to be in that place with him, to be there, Pappa says, not to look on it with clever thoughts and a lot of talk. But I was trying to help, I say. And Pappa fixes his eyes on me for a long moment, then says in the quietest voice: You'll only make him feel more alone like that.

What can I do then, Pappa? You can't do anything. Patience, Pappa says. All you can do is wait, he says. Sit by the tree and wait, like the cattle in the meadow, Pappa says, wait for him to come to you.

I've been so naive. M's only thirty-five and much closer age-wise to the boy cowering before that terrifying drunken figure I saw mirrored in his eyes. He's got no one to turn to. He hasn't even got himself, alone as he is in his flat in the evenings with the curtains drawn, doing as best he can, running a firm with two men working for him, slogging away from morning until night, smoking weed in order to relax, going for walks with the dog he kicks and loves, but he's got no one beside him in all his images of terror and degradation and fear, he's got no language, no framework or system, no shape or form, and who am I to come turning everything on its head, when this is all he has to hold on to, this understanding, no matter how insane I think it is, no matter how obvious it is to me that it's the little boy who's in need of sympathy and solidarity, the little boy who needs the grown-up M to bend down and open his arms and say, Come on, little one, let's run, let's take off, we'll go away, as far away as we can, and never come back here, ever again.

I leave Pappa to himself and once again everything's turned upside down. I thought I was doing something to help M, but all I did was hurt him even more. Alone. Ten days have passed, maybe more. I text him. I tell him all this. I say I'm sorry.

//

Perhaps Judith's a clearer picture of me in the novel than the first-person narrator is, my notebook says.

The floating jetty stretching out over the water in Minneapolis in the late hours of evening, into the night. The water lies there, the forest on the other side surrounding it, a dark, arcing curve below, and then above, above the treetops, a hint of purple, a band of blue before the great night sky. The stars up there reflect in the water's surface, little blurs of light. All is still. And there is no more.

Pappa tells me about his uncle E who was a heart surgeon, he used to hit my sister, Pappa says. And then there was Irma's husband, these are people they knew when I was a child, he beat his wife too, he beat her with pots and things, I think I remember, and I tell him that too, and Pappa's breathing clogs up, we'll talk about something else, I say, all this is getting to be too much, and so we natter about something else, I can't remember what, and it settles, his coughing, but what I don't know, and I don't ask him either, is what he calls it himself, the way he behaved towards Mamma, the things he did when I'd be lying there listening in my bed. Wasn't that hitting? If it wasn't, then what was it? Has he just erased it from his mind, has he called it something else, or does he think of it as something quite different? I text Mamma and ask her, put it to her exactly like that, I tell her what Pappa says about those other men, that he says they hit their wives, or beat them, but how would she refer to what he did to her? She doesn't reply, sends a smiley in reply to something else, but about this she's totally silent and it's always been her way, not to say anything, not to talk about it, as if it doesn't exist to her then, or doesn't hurt as much, what do I know, and I think to myself she won't ever answer me on that. What was it like, exactly? The only thing I can get a handle on is what it's like for me, now.

There's a white rose made from a serviette hanging from the door when I step out of the lift with my suitcase. The next day there's a red one and a silver heart-shaped balloon attached to the street sign outside the entrance. They flutter softly in the breeze and they're us, M and me, they touch and collide, repel each other, then come together once more, rubbing gently against each other.

Can we meet? Some days have passed and we agree on the corner of the little park just across from my building, my arms are throbbing and suddenly he's there, his white shirt in the dark, his head lowered, he squints up at me with caution, as if he doesn't know quite what to expect, doesn't he realise how happy I am to see him, that he's not the one who needs to be afraid, I am.

I pause in front of the mirror on my way to the laundry room with my gym clothes, pause and look at myself, and I don't know her.

Where is she? How can I find her? Be with her? How can I get her to feel less alone?

It's as if I'm not really taking myself seriously. As if I don't believe. It's clearest to me in the evenings, when I'm tired, exhausted. No one wants me. The eyes I see in the mirror, why do I love them less than I feel I love M, when I look into his eyes?

//

I'm not getting anywhere with my novel. I'm waiting. Week after week, I wait.

I amble by the canal with Camilla, her pregnant belly, it won't be long now, she's wearing her red hat, the sun's beating down and there are the toes of our shoes against the white asphalt, I tell her I get so desperately afraid sometimes of losing M. Not just of losing him, but of being abandoned, or more precisely: not making the grade. That what he really wants is something else, someone else. I get afraid that I'm not worth having. Afraid of being unloved.

I can't get anything done in this frame of mind, I say, it's like I'm paralysed, I can hardly breathe. Hm, she says. We pass through the shade of a tree, branches overhanging the high wall, and she narrows her eyes as if trying to focus on something far away. Then she asks what it was like when Mamma went away.

I've never thought about it.

I've told her about Mamma leaving us to get some more qualifications. From Tana to Oslo, in 1973, the college of social work at the Diakonhjemmet hospital. She'd had three children and wasn't yet twenty-five years old. She didn't go away because she didn't want us, because she was sick of being a mother. Is what I write.

I don't believe it. If she hadn't wanted to leave us, then surely they'd have organised things so we could go together, all of us, so that we three kids and both dogs and the budgie could go too. And Pappa. Wouldn't that have been the case? Isn't that the bottom line?

But she went on her own.

And I've never addressed it. I've worked with myself a lot relating to the time when I would hear them fighting, from when I was ten or eleven until they got divorced when I was eighteen. And I've made myself able to go in there and be with her, sit with her, and eventually take her by the hand, the young girl in her bed, lead her out of that room and take her with me.

But that little girl of three and a half. Nothing.

The only thing I remember is from a photograph. It's from the Esso station at Rustefjelbma where the bus stops, the bus that's to take Mamma to the airport, and we're there all three of us, all three children, and probably the dogs too, and it's 21 August (Pappa tells me), grey and rainy, and the bus stopping, the noise it makes, the sigh, and Mamma getting on, I see her legs, her boots, go up the steps. And then the door must have closed again and the bus must have driven away.

Then what?

After that photograph, nothing. It's completely dark. I can't remember.

That's why I've never addressed it. I had nothing to address. I've always known that was how Mamma left. But I've never had anything I could hold on to, have always thought it couldn't have been that bad if I can't remember anything. If there was something important in all that, wouldn't it have made itself known?

The next thing I remember is from Rovaniemi. November the 15th and minus 43 degrees, Pappa says. Mamma's come up a few days before, we're going south, all of us together, they've lined the back of the white estate car with reindeer skins for us and the dogs, and when we get to Rovaniemi we're going to stay at a hotel. They carry our things in from the car in stages, Mamma and Pappa, through the cold, the snow, the darkness, they've brought the plants from the living room in cardboard boxes, I see nothing, my memory has switched off, for four months everything's dark, and then, the next thing I see, as if someone has suddenly turned on the light, we're sitting at a round table with a big table-cloth hanging down in the hotel restaurant, and there's piano music and people twirling around, and the air thick with smoke. And I'm afraid. There's something ominous. I don't know what it is.

Pappa tells me they prepared us, like a pair of conscientious schoolteachers, they take us with them to Nesseby to meet the ladies who're going to look after us when Mamma goes away. I suppose it was ingrained in me from my mother, Pappa puts in a text, that her daughters, and therefore your mother likewise, should have an education, so we knew that was how it would have to be. And of course I couldn't agree more, I'm really glad Mamma got herself an education, I really am.

But what about that little girl left behind when the bus drove away?

Mamma's chosen something else. Something other than me. And it's not just for today. It's tomorrow as well. She's not coming back.

This is for good.

When Pappa writes *That was how it was*, then that was how it was. They had no plans for us to follow on to Oslo. She went away, and that was it. And they knew she wasn't coming back either. It was like it or lump it. Lying there, trying to sleep when that's how it is. Waking up the next day, the sense that there's no prospect of change, no hope, no promise, none, and there never will be, and she's gone away because she doesn't want me.

That feeling of permanence, that loving someone is to exist in a state of permanence which is a kind of death. Without movement, without change. An unyielding standstill. Which feels unbearable, I want only to remove myself from it, to do something, alter it. The relief if it would only end. I never understood where that feeling came from, until now.

It feels impossible to go into that dark span of time. It's thick and compact, and I'm scared stiff, it feels like extinction.

But then, in the days that follow, it begins to unravel and gradually I'm able to see. The images fade up, quietly, from within.

Two images. The first is from the kitchen, a little girl, she's sitting in the window looking out.

The second is a hole, a well, in the kitchen, this one too, the whole image is this well and inside the well is only black and unending emptiness. And the girl is in the hole. She's holding on to the edge with both hands. If she lets go she'll fall.

I remember NO. I remember it from some point in those four months. I've written about it before, in *Week 43*, Mamma phones from Oslo, the black receiver handed to me, Mamma at the other end and me somewhere in the house at the mouth of the river, people, we're in a room and there are other people there, not just my brothers and Pappa, a smoky room, voices, and then the telephone, the receiver in my hand, me screaming, NO.

No was the only thing I could *do*. Because I couldn't do anything. Saying no was the only thing I had. There was nothing else.

Like when I left my publishers when there was a change of editor at the start of the millennium. I've always thought it was to do with different views on literature, I didn't agree with how they were going to manage the literary side and I left to protect my books from a narrative I couldn't subscribe to. I still believe that was right. But for the first time now I see where that massive emotional thrust was coming from: my editor had left me. She'd packed in her job, the first editor I had, the woman who'd spotted me and picked me out and who wanted me. Now she didn't want me any more. She just upped and left. And what I did then was to say no, again. I left too. It was terrible and I felt like I was excluding myself, which I was too, but it was the only thing I could do. And it's only now as I'm writing this that it becomes clear to me why it felt like I had no choice.

I become aware of the laughter. We lived in a psychiatric care home for boys, they were together with us all the time, Pappa ran the place. They laugh at her, the boys on the sofa, on the chairs, presumably they were doing something together, playing cards maybe, or Yatzy, when the telephone rang and it was from Oslo, and all of a sudden Pappa's little girl yells into the receiver, No, and maybe it's so fierce they don't know what to do other than laugh. Whatever, she can't be having it. Because that no is her, and there they are laughing at what is her. As if she doesn't exist, as if what she is isn't important, and has no worth.

Her no: LISTEN TO ME. Such an immense force in her. And I realise that's when it happens. That's when it takes shape inside her, so clearly, so unmistakably, suddenly I see that she's me, the writer, she's in the very core of me. I remember when I made my debut and in the years that followed, whenever I was asked about why I wrote, I'd always say, emphatically: *It's not true. I don't believe it. It's not the way it is.* But where it came from, that thrust, I didn't know. All I knew was that it was all I had. That it was me.

And it is. But it's not the only thing. There's more. There's that other girl too. She's in the kitchen, sitting in the window, looking out. The river and the light.

All of a sudden I realise she thought Mamma was so beautiful. Mamma was twenty-four when she went away. I think I must have liked looking at her very much. She was kind. I can't remember her ever shouting at me. She must have been a very kind young woman. The photograph from the table in Ørsta, the hardness in Farmor's eyes, my anxious brother, Mamma's in that photo too, leaning slightly back towards the camera, towards Pappa, there's the hint of a smile on her face, as if there was an openness between them, a joy, and there's something so soft in her there, her cheeks, in her eyes, youth and the newness of all things, and the same softness my own daughter has, which I've never been able to recognise in myself.

And I've always thought I don't love Mamma, but now I wonder if that too is love, finding Mamma so captivating. And I understand why I've always thought, and written, time and again, in book after book, that there's a tenderness in beauty. Little me, who loved her mamma, and the feeling that she was the finest of all for me.

And then she went away and was gone.

I see that I've wanted to make myself like that. Like her. That the hairstyle I finally settled into, more than fifteen years ago now, after having been shaven-headed, dyed red, curly, black, cropped and then bleached, that the way I've worn my hair since then is the same way Mamma wore hers when she left. High at the neck, the diagonal sweep over the line of the cheeks. And I understand why I can't see myself with a rounder body. Because Mamma's body wasn't like that. Mamma was super thin, she dieted every time she'd given birth, ate only a boiled egg and was thin again in a jiffy. Thin and beautiful she must have been to me. And have I been trying to make myself into her? To be like her, to get back what I lost? So that I have it with me, what went away, which I can't entrust to anyone else, and so I've made myself the same way, so I won't have to lose anything again.

11

M jumps out of the van on the other side of the street. It's morning, *where are you*, he asks over the phone, and I tell him the street, I'm out walking: But that's where I am too! And then the slam of the door and he's standing there, his fine and slender body, I cross over, so happy he is, he presses his face against my neck, leans back against the side of the van and draws me close to him, away from the traffic.

I've never, not once, believed anyone loved me. If someone's given me a tender look, I've dismissed it, never let it nourish me or give me warmth. Because before I know it, it's happened, automatic and hard the angry one in me pushes to the front and like a soldier takes command and tells me: It's not true. Don't get fooled. She wants only to protect that little girl in the kitchen, that soft and watchful little girl, and what she says is: Never again will anyone be allowed to captivate you only to up and leave. But it's led to me shutting myself out.

Something alters. Now that I can see the two of them separate from each other, the no-girl and the girl in the window, existing each in their own right, it means I can separate them emotionally too. I can calm the angry one down and say now I'm grown up, now it's me looking after you, in the kitchen. And I can be there then, in the kitchen with the little one, looking out. I sit myself next to her and we look out together. She's so quiet and kind.

The urge to drink subsides.

Soft evenings in the darkness on the balcony, M's low voice, I listen, at the centre of everything where only we are, I see the lights below us and in the distance. He makes me a gift of a ring. It's too big, so I wear it on my forefinger, a thin thread of gold topped by a heart. We'll get married in Las Vegas, he says, and means it.

And all of a sudden I see Pappa's eyes, he shuffles to the door to see me out after I've eaten all the prawns, all he's done for me, the things he's said, in the couple of hours we've been sitting in front of the TV, crossing the floor in his stocking feet, unsteady and frail he stands in the hall, and as I close the door behind me, his eyes then, the way they look at me, and all of a sudden I realise, for the first time, what it is I see: his eyes are full of love.

Now he's got the Defender it becomes so tangible and real, we talk about it in the kitchen or when M picks me up in the van and we go off fishing somewhere, we talk about it in line at the supermarket checkout, or watching his dog as she dashes about, how happy she is, running about like that even though she's old, in the green field, and of course she'll come too, when we leave Milan behind, when at last it's summer again, and M works in the garage in the evenings, he's got hold of a big container so we'll have fresh water, and together we make a long trip to pick up one of those tents for the roof, it's raining when we get there and we have to open everything out to make sure it all works, there's a mattress inside ready for use, all you have to do is unfold the tent, it opens like a fan, and there we are, at the mouth of the river, the Red Mountains in the distance, inside me I know exactly where we are, we turn off onto the unmade track and carry on down, the dry tufty grass, and we pull up at the bottom by the rocks, before the river and the sandbanks, we light a fire, and when evening comes we put the tent up and climb into our sleeping bags, we sleep, and when it's morning we unzip them and climb out, the delta flooded with the light of a brand new day, the dog dashing about, and we sit there together, on the roof looking out, and we're there, together, and that's all there is.

But it doesn't last. Why can't it last? Why can't it just work out?

//

M's doing a hundred and sixty. I'm not thinking, saying nothing, my brothers and I are on the back seat, and there's snow and pine trees, snow all around, and he brakes abruptly causing the car to skid sideways, and then it's everybody out, all the doors flung open, the sudden cold, Out, he shouts, but no one moves, not Mamma, no one says anything, and the dog cowers in my lap. I hate you. M looks at me. I know, I say. He's pulled into the services, there's a beer on the table in front of him, it's dark, it's late, we're on our way back to Milan.

We've been away by the sea and he's been distant all day, as if he'd rather be on his own, and before we leave, it's Sunday evening, he's lying on the bed with his phone, I've tidied the kitchen and I come in and sit down on the other side of the bed, I reach out and run a finger over his thigh and say, cautiously, that I'm missing some closeness, that's all, but it's enough to make him explode, a torrent of harshness and anger, everything that's been wrong since we left home on the Friday, he can't have a moment to himself, he rants, and now this, it's set him off, he's well away now and won't stop, we'd planned to go out and have dinner there by the sea before setting off home, but that's not going to happen now, what I said has ruined everything, he tells me, and abruptly he jumps to his feet and then it's bags packed, the dog in the back, and off we go.

Why can't I just leave? Leave M. What is it that's stopping me? Isn't it supposed to be love? Isn't love supposed to be something good, something warm and safe? But it's not like that, not with M. With M everything's up in the air, all the time. What is it then that ties me? What's strongest in our relationship is fear. With M I'm afraid, the whole time. The way I was afraid the whole time I was growing up. Is fear a bond? Is fear as strong as softness, kindness?

At the round table with the red notebook, if someone had done something, if my brothers told them about it, or I did, that someone had done something to us, whatever, I can't remember, pushed or said something, an injustice. It was never: That wasn't very nice of them, the cheek of it, no, it was always the opposite, it was always: Think about that boy who lives on his own with his mother, the woman who cleans for the council and who's always shouting whenever she opens her mouth, think about that. And I'd think about their run-down house with the dark windows, what it would be like to have to go home to such a place every day after school. I'd be frustrated too if that was me, Pappa says, and his eyes fix on me, it's no wonder, it's got to come out somehow. And I understand that, I do, and that's the end of it then. Then it's Pappa who's angry. But he's actually only frustrated. His mother thrashing him in the barn, and now it's Mamma who's not listening. He jumps to his feet, he too, and shouts, he slams his fist down on the table. We cry. It's once a week, or twice. Of course I understand.

Patience, Pappa says. But who's being patient with me?

I'm in the hall, in the Oslo flat, Pappa comes out of the kitchen behind me, Mamma from the side, darting in front of me, her work stuffed into a carrier bag, and she tears the front door open, I'm seventeen years old, she goes out the door, I stand between them, she runs down the stairs in a hurry so Pappa can't get to her, *he never lays a hand on me.* She's outside and away, and then he lays a hand on me, he grabs me by the arms and twists me round and pushes me back through the hall, through the kitchen, into my room, over to the bed, and he presses me down onto the bed, and he must have stood over me then, pressing and holding me there.

I can't remember. He must have let go, and left the room.

The fear: there are no boundaries any more, in that other person. It's the place where the plain lies wide open with the wind blowing across, right through to the other side where there's only emptiness forever, and you'll never come back and find the road ever again.

How did it go? No one asks, not Mamma, not once. Pappa comes to stay with me in Milan. He's already found a place to sit in arrivals when I come up from the train, on a bench with his wheelie case, phone in hand, his stick leaned against his thigh. On the way out he tries to take note, signs to follow when he goes back. He's staying a week. Pappa, I tell him, you don't need to think about that. I'll come with you.

I've had wi-fi installed for when he comes. The week before, I buy a TV so we've got a big screen to watch films on together in the evenings. We establish a routine, I get up shortly after six and drink coffee and tea and sit on the sofa writing. At nine he comes in and sits down in a chair by the window, he reads the news on the computer, he's brought a little gadget with him, a key fob authenticator, so he can log on to NRK. When it's about Ukraine he turns the sound up, Putin's launched another assault, it's the day the helicopter crashes on the outskirts of Kyiv, the minister of internal affairs and several others, children among them, are killed, it crashes into a housing block where there's a nursery school. He makes himself coffee, doesn't want me fetching and bringing, and at half past ten he fries some bacon along with two eggs. I do half an hour's YouTube yoga on the living room floor, go to the gym every other day, Nordic and weights, Pappa'll be sitting in the same place when I get back, in the chair, watching the news. Once I've showered we go out, he with his stick and his scarf, a woolly hat. We walk by the canal to the little church, jump on a tram halfway there. He has ambitions about walking himself into shape after a period at home with a cold, but it's like I'm exhausted before I've even started, he says, wait until you get old. I take a picture of him every day, sometimes a selfie of us both, and send it to Mamma. Enjoy, she replies with a heart-face emoji. He's glad to hear of our trip to the North this coming summer, it's almost as if I'm going with you, he says with a smile he directs at M. But for the most part we're on our own, Pappa and I, neither of them's much of a talker, and anyway they can't speak English. But he talks to me, about all sorts of things, he tells me about when he was little, about China and his mother, about them enrolling him at the Diakonhjemmet, she and his father, so he could train in nursing and social ministry, Gaza was a continuation of his military service after he completed that training. I ask him about when they laid the foundation of the house in Tana, he and my brother: It was minus twenty degrees the day I started, Pappa says, what do you mean *you*, I say, my brother was helping you, but no, Pappa says, that job I did on my own. He has his first gin and tonic of the day, picks out the slice of lemon and drops it in my glass of water, it's nearly three o'clock by now and we sit at the nearby café where I sometimes go to see people and read. I definitely remember him laying that foundation with you, working away in the evenings, I say, without saying he was *forced*, even though he was, but Pappa just shakes his head. We sit there a while and our food arrives, chicken breast, and Pappa's surprised and pleased that it's not too dry, we joke about our teeth, the ones we're missing, and implants. Afterwards I order a coffee, he's still got half his G&T. We're quiet, that dark pit. It was a hell of a job, Pappa says, as if to himself. It's odd you can't remember him helping you, I say. But he didn't, Pappa says again, he did it on his own. He's not usually one to get mixed up. I'll ask him, I say, and text my brother in England. He replies inside a minute: *Yes, I remember that well.* We get to our feet, Pappa pays the bill, he insists, his hat on squint, his stick leaned against the counter. When we're outside again he looks at me and asks, How old could he have been? We start walking towards home. Twelve, I tell him. And Pappa shakes his head. To think I could forget such a thing, he says. All I remember is myself.

11

I sit down on the edge of the bed and say to Pappa as he grips the girl and holds her down: No, no, I say. You mustn't. And Pappa lets go. Then he starts crying. The girl puts her arms around him.

No, come on, that's no good.

Start again. I sit down on the edge of the bed and say to Pappa: No. You mustn't. And then Pappa lets go and starts crying. Dear little Pappa, the boy he once was, all on his own up on the fell, all night long with his fishing rod at the beck. But instead of looking at Pappa I look at the girl. He can just sit there.

The same thing at the door. I'm standing beside the girl. I'm saying No, Pappa, you can't. Let go, I say. Mamma out through the door, gone. It's just the two of us. No. And the way he realises then, and lets go. He lets go of me, and he sinks to his knees and starts crying. And again, me going over, the girl goes over to him and bends down and puts her arms around him.

No, I say to myself. No!

Again. I'm standing beside the girl and Pappa grips her arms. And instead of looking at Pappa, this time I look at her. I look only at her. It's as if my gaze is drawn towards Pappa the whole time, but I have to resist and focus only on the girl, she's the one I've got to look at now. And then he starts crying, but it won't help. I look at the girl. She looks at me, almost as if she doesn't quite believe it, almost as if it isn't true. But it is. I look at her. I say: It's you and me now. I'm here now.

//

Then I can do the same thing with M. I shift my gaze. I look at me, instead of looking at him. I see myself sitting across the table from him. M's been wanting us to go to Amsterdam for such a long time, he rolls a joint, we're sitting in a coffee shop and have just done some mushrooms, it was me who wanted to do mushrooms, but it hasn't started working yet. He says the girl behind me is looking at him, he could have her straight away if he wanted, he says, she's all ready for him, and I turn round and look at her, a young girl in a yellow sweater, she couldn't have been more ordinary, which only humiliates me further, making me jealous of someone so plain, someone who doesn't even look good, and the fact that it works, it makes me feel so low about myself, I feel low about myself already, there's no tenderness between us, what am I even doing here, all I am is afraid. And the mushrooms make me even more afraid, and then they throw us out because you're not allowed to do mushrooms there, they've noticed the empty box on the table, so we go back to the hotel, climb the steep staircase to the narrow room under the sloping roof, M lies innermost against the wall with his back to me, and then it kicks in. I see only one thing, over and over. M has me kept like an animal, in a wire cage. He stands outside the cage with a whip in his hand, taunting, laughing, but it's not what he does, it's the feeling. I see nothing else, just that one image, the whole time. Or, I do see something else. I see myself from the outside. Brief little flashes. I see the woman of fifty-three in her coat and scarf next to the young man with glasses, I see her riding behind him on a bike, I see her going in and out of smoke-filled dives. That dignified, grown-up woman, it's so obvious she's out on the town. Then all of a sudden M shoves me aside, he scrambles out of bed to the toilet and throws up. He comes and lies down again, curls into a ball. I say nothing about what I'm seeing. I think about texting someone, but I don't want to frighten them. I know it'll wear off. I look at the time. Only a few hours more. I don't know how many hours have passed when M says he's hungry and gets dressed. I'm incapable of going anywhere and ask him to bring me something back. The relief when he leaves the room. What do I do now. I've seen something I can't unsee. I text someone I know who does this kind of thing, and ask if the mushrooms can be lying. *You're* not lying, she texts back. The mushrooms just let you see what you already know. What do I do now, we've a whole day yet before we go home, what the hell do I do now. I phone my friend, the crisis-centre friend, I put the earbud into my ear and he holds my hand with his voice. Keep a level head and don't provoke him, that's the plan. We're still talking when M gets back, McDonald's, I hang up. You've got something white here, something foamy, M says, and traces a finger over the corner of his mouth.

Milan, I bring my flight forwards, leave for Oslo the day after. At the bagage reclaim, as the luggage starts dumping onto the carousel, he phones. I answer. It's over, I tell him. For good.

I stand at the table in the coffee shop and instead of looking at M, I look at the girl. I see she's the adult me. But when I think about her she's just a girl. I see how afraid she is, how alone, I see how sad she is with the shaven-headed man as he crumbles the resin into the tobacco, the cigarette paper held between the fingers and thumb of his other hand, the cardboard roach tucked behind his ear and his eyes seeking out that other girl behind her back. I stand quite collected beside her. Come on, I say. You're not meant to be here.

//

In Oslo, on my way up the stairs from the shopping centre basement where I've had a key cut, my helmet in one hand, I feel the strap of my backpack slide down my shoulder, and immediately someone comes up behind me and helps it back into place. There you go, he says, already on his way past, and I look at him, it can't be, it is: Jørgen, I burst out. He turns and smiles. His hair's not red any more, it's fair, thinner, it must be fifteen years at least since that time in the prison. We go outside together. He stands with me as I unlock my bike. We hug each other. I cycle away.

Judith has on her brown dress, it still fits, slightly too big if anything, which it wasn't before, long puff sleeves, she pulls down the zip and the dress slips from her body, piles at her feet. She goes out into the water, feet upon stones, and going forwards she is seventeen again, her hair is red and curly again and her breasts are small and unused, and as she wades so too the eagle rises, as if out of Judith herself, it's possible to see them both at the same time, Judith stepping out and the bird lifting into the sky where the trees come together and end, the clearness and the blue, Judith and the eagle high above.

Dear readers,

As a publisher of shamelessly literary books, in addition to bookshop sales, we rely on subscriptions from people like you in order to publish in line with our values.

All of our subscribers:

- receive a first edition copy of each of the books they subscribe to
- are thanked by name at the end of our subscriber-supported books

BECOME A SUBSCRIBER, OR GIVE A SUBSCRIPTION TO A FRIEND

Visit andotherstories.org/subscribe to help make our books happen. You can subscribe to a selection of the books we're in the process of making. To purchase books we have already published, we urge you to support your local or favourite bookshop and order directly from them – the often unsung heroes of publishing.

OTHER WAYS TO GET INVOLVED

If you'd like to know about our upcoming books and events, please follow us via:

- our monthly newsletter, sign up here: andotherstories.org
- Facebook: facebook.com/AndOtherStoriesBooks
- Instagram: @andotherpics
- TikTok: @andotherbooktok
- X: @andothertweets
- Our blog: andotherstories.org/ampersand

THIS BOOK WAS MADE POSSIBLE THANKS TO THE SUPPORT OF

Aaron McEnery
Aaron Schneider
Abigail Walton
Adam Lenson
Adriel Levine
Ajay Sharma
Al Ullman
Alan McMonagle
Alasdair Cross
Albert Puente
Alex Fleming
Alex Liebman
Alex Ramsey
Alex (Anna) Turner
Alexandra German
Alexandra Stewart
Alexandria Levitt
Ali Boston
Ali Ersahin
Ali Smith
Ali Usman
Alice Carrick-Smith
Alice Wilkinson
Aliki Giakou
Alison Hardy
Allan & Mo Tennant
Alyssa Rinaldi
Amado Floresca
Amaia Gabantxo
Amanda
Amanda Milanetti
Amber Casiot
Amelia Dowe
Amine Hamadache
Amitav Hajra
Amos Hintermann
Amy and Jamie
Amy Hatch
Amy Lloyd
Amy Sousa
Amy Tabb
Ana Novak
Andrea Barlien
Andrea Larsen
Andrea Oyarzabal Koppes
Andreas Zbinden
Andrew Burns
Andrew Marston
Andrew Martino
Andrew McCallum
Andrew Milam
Andrew Place
Andrew Place
Andrew Reece
Andrew Rego
Andrew Wright
Angus Walker
Anna Finneran
Anna French
Anna Gibson
Anna Hawthorne
Anna Holmes
Anna Kornilova
Anna Milsom
Anne Edyvean
Anne Frost
Anne Germanacos
Anne-Marie Renshaw
Anne Ryden
Anne Willborn
Annette Hamilton
Annie McDermott
Anonymous
Ant Cotton
Anthony Fortenberry
Antonia Saske
Antony Pearce
April Hernandez
Archie Davies
Aron Trauring
Asako Serizawa
Audrey Holmes
Audrey Small
Barbara Mellor
Barbara Spicer
Barry Norton
Becky Matthewson
Ben Buchwald
Ben Schofield
Ben Thornton
Ben Walter
Benjamin Judge
Benjamin Pester
Benjamin Heanue
Beth Heim de Bera
Bianca Winter
Bill Fletcher
Billy-Ray Belcourt
Björn Dade
Blazej Jedras
Brandon Clar
Brendan Dunne
Brett Parker
Briallen Hopper
Brian Anderson
Brian Byrne
Brian Callaghan
Brian Isabelle
Brian Smith
Bridget Maddison
Bridget Prentice
Brittany Redgate
Brooks Williams
Buck Johnston & Camp Bosworth
Burkhard Fehsenfeld
Buzz Poole
Caitlin Farr Hurst
Caitlin Halpern
Caleb Bedford
Callie Steven
Cameron Adams
Camilla Imperiali
Carmen Smith
Carole Parkhouse
Carolina Pineiro
Caroline Kim
Caroline Montanari
Caroline Musgrove
Caroline West
Carrie Brogoitti
Caryn Cochran
Catharine Braithwaite
Catherine Connell
Catherine Fisher
Catherine Jacobs
Catherine Lambert
Catherine McBeth
Catherine Williamson
Catherine Tandy
Cathryn Siegal-Bergman
Cathy Leow
Cecilia Rossi
Cecilia Uribe
Ceri Lumley-Sim
Cerileigh Guichelaar
Chandler Sanchez
Charles Fernyhough
Charles Heiner
Charles Rowe
Charles Dee Mitchell
Charlie Mitchell
Charlie Small
Charlotte Coulthard
Charlotte Holtam
Charlotte Ryland
Charlotte Whittle
Chelsey Blankenship
Cherilyn Elston
China Miéville
Chris Clamp
Chris Johnstone
Chris Lintott
Chris Potts
Chris Senior

Chris Stevenson
Christina Sarver
Christine Bartels
Christopher Fox
Christopher Stout
Cian McAulay
Ciara Callaghan
Claire Brooksby
Claire Mackintosh
Claire Williams
Clare Wilkins
Claudia Mazzoncini
Cliona Quigley
Colin Denyer
Colin Hewlett
Colin Matthews
Collin Brooke
Conor McMeel
Courtney Daniel
Courtney Lilly
Craig Kennedy
Cynthia De La Torre
Cyrus Massoudi
Daisy Savage
Dale Wisely
Dalia Cavazos
Daniel Cossai
Daniel Hahn
Daniel Sanford
Daniel Syrovy
Daniela Steierberg
Darcie Vigliano
Darren Boyling
Darren Gillen
Darryll Rogers
Darya Lisouskaya
Dave Appleby
Dave Lander
David Alderson
David Anderson
David Ball
David Eales
David Gould
David Gray
David Greenlaw
David Gunnarsson
David Hebblethwaite
David Higgins
David Johnson-Davies
David Kaus
David F Long
David Morris
David Richardson
David Shriver
David Smith
David Smith
David Toft
David Wacks
Dawn Walter
Dean Taucher
Deb Unferth
Debbie Enever
Debbie Pinfold
Deborah Gardner
Deborah Green
Deborah McLean
Debra Manskey
Declan O'Driscoll
Denis Larose
Denise Brown
Derek Meins
Diane Hamilton
Diane Josefowicz
Diarmuid Hickey
Dinesh Prasad
Dominic Nolan
Dominic Bailey
Dominick Santa Cattarina
Dominique Brocard
Dominique Hudson
Doris Duhennois
Dorothy Bottrell
Douglas Smoot
Dugald Mackie
Duncan Chambers
Duncan Clubb
Duncan Macgregor
Dyanne Prinsen
Ebba Tornérhielm
Ed Smith
Edward Champion
Ekaterina Beliakova
Eleanor Maier
Elif Kolcuoglu
Elina Zicmane
Eliza Mood
Elizabeth Atkinson
Elizabeth Balmain
Elizabeth Braswell
Elizabeth Draper
Elizabeth Franz
Elizabeth Guss
Elizabeth Eva Leach
Elizabeth Rice
Elizabeth Seals
Elizabeth Sieminski
Ella Sabiduria
Ellen Agnew
Ellie Goddard
Emiliano Gomez
Emma Bielecki
Emma Louise Grove
Emma Post
Emma Teale
Emma Wakefield
Erin Cameron Allen
Ethan White
Ethan Wood
Evelyn Reis
Ewan Tant
Fawzia Kane
Fay Barrett
Faye Williams
Felicity Le Quesne
Felix Valdivieso
Finbarr Farragher
Fiona Mozley
Fiona Quinn
Fiona Wilson
Fran Sanderson
Frances Gillon
Frances Harvey
Francesca Brooks
Frank Pearson
Frank Rodrigues
Frank van Orsouw
Gabriel Garcia
Gabriella Roncone
Garland Gardner
Gavin Aitchison
Gavin Collins
Gawain Espley
Gemma Alexander
Gemma Hopkins
Geoff Thrower
Geoffrey Urland
George McCaig
George Stanbury
George Wilkinson
Georgia Panteli
Gerry Craddock
Gillian Grant
Gillian Spencer
Gina Filo
Glen Bornais
Glenn Russell
Gloria Gunn
Gordon Cameron
Graham Blenkinsop
Graham R Foster
Grainne Otoole
Grant Ray-Howett
Hadil Balzan
Halina Schiffman-Shilo
Hannah Harford-Wright
Hannah Levinson
Hannah Jane Lownsbrough
Hannah Madonia
Hannah Rapley
Hans Lazda
Harriet Stiles
Haydon Spenceley
Heidi James
Helen Alexander
Helen Berry
Helen Mort

Henrike Laehnemann
Holly Down
Howard Robinson
Hugh Shipley
Hum Drum Press Amy Gowen
Hyoung-Won Park
Ian Betteridge
Ian McMillan
Ian Mond
Ian Randall
Ian Whiteley
Ida Grochowska
Ilya Markov
Inbar Haramati
Ines Alfano
Inga Gaile
Irene Mansfield
Irina Tzanova
Isabella Weibrecht
J Shmotkina
Jack Brown
Jaclyn Schultz
Jacob Musser
Jacqueline Haskell
Jacqueline Lademann
Jacqueline Vint
Jake Baldwinson
James Avery
James Beck
James Crossley
James Cubbon
James Kinsley
James Lehmann
James Leonard
James Portlock
James Richards
James Ruland
James Saunders
James Scudamore
James Thomson
James Higgs
James Silvestro
Jan Hicks
Jane Dolman
Jane Leuchter
Jane Roberts
Jane Roberts
Jane Woollard
Janet Digby
Janis Carpenter
Jason Montano
Jason Timermanis
J E Crispin
Jeanne Guyon
Jeff Collins
Jen Hardwicke
Jennifer Fain
Jennifer Frost
Jennifer Mills
Jennifer Fosket
Jennifer Yanoschak
Jenny Huth
Jeremy Koenig
Jeremy Sabol
Jerome Mersky
Jess Decamps
Jess Wood
Jessica Gately
Jessica Kibler
Jessica Queree
Jethro Soutar
Jill Harrison
Jo Clarke
Jo Heinrich
Jo Lateu
Joanna Luloff
Joanna Trachtenberg
Joao Pedro Bragatti Winckler
Jodie Adams
Joel Hulseman
Joelle Young
Johannah May Black
Johannes Holmqvist
Johannes Menzel
Johannes Georg Zipp
John Betteridge
John Bogg
John Carnahan
John Conway
John Gent
John Hodgson
John Kelly
John Miller
John Purser
John Reid
John Shaw
John Steigerwald
John Walsh
John Whiteside
John Winkelman
John Wyatt
Jon Riches
Jonah Benton
Jonathan Blaney
Jonathan Leaver
Jonathan Woollen
Joni Chan
Jonny Anderson
Jonny Kiehlmann
Jordana Carlin
José Echeverría Vega
Joseph Thomas
Josephine Glöckner
Josh Glitz
Joshua Briggs
Joshua Davis
Judith Gruet-Kaye
Julia Rochester
Julia Von Dem Knesebeck
Julie Atherton
Juliette Loesch
Junius Hoffman
Jupiter Jones
Juraj Janik
Kaarina Hollo
Kalina Rose
Karen Gilbert
Karen Mahinski
Karl Chwe
Katarzyna Bartoszynska
Kate Beswick
Kate Rizzo
Katharine Robbins
Katherine Sotejeff-Wilson
Kathryn Edwards
Kathryn Williams
Kati Hallikainen
Katie Cooke
Katie Freeman
Katie Grant
Katie Zegar
Katrina Mayson
Katy Robinson
Keith Walker
Kelly Hydrick
Kelsey Grashoff
Kenneth Blythe
Kent McKernan
Kerry Broderick
Kieran Cutting
Kieran Rollin
Kieron James
Kirsten Benites
Kitty Golden
K L Ee
Kris Ann Trimis
Kris Fernandez-Everett
Kristen Tcherneshoff
Kristen Tracey
Kristin Djuve
Krystale Tremblay-Moll
Krystine Phelps
Kurt Navratil
Kyle Pienaar
Lana Selby
Lara Holtz
Laura Ling
Laura Murphy
Laura Zlatos
Lauren Pout
Lauren Rea
Lauren Trestler
Laurence Laluyaux
Leah Binns
Leda Brittenham
Lee Harbour
Leona Iosifidou
Lex Orgera
Liliana Lobato

Lilie Weaver
Linda Jones
Linda Whittle
Lindsay Brammer
Lisa Hess
Liz Clifford
Liz Ladd
Lorna Bleach
Louis Lewarne
Louise Aitken
Louise Evans
Louise Jolliffe
Lucinda Smith
Lucy Moffatt
Luiz Cesar Peres
Luke Healey
Luke Murphy
Lydia Syson
Lynda Graham
Lyndia Thomas
Lynn Fung
Lynn Grant
Lynn Martin
Mack McKenna
Madalyn Marcus
Maeve Lambe
Maggie Livesey
Margaret Dillow
Margaret Jull Costa
Marian Zelman
Mariann Wang
Mari-Liis Calloway
Marina Castledine
Mark Grainger
Mark Reynolds
Mark Sargent
Mark Sheets
Mark Sztyber
Mark Tronco
Mark Troop
Martha Wakenshaw
Martin Price
Martin Eric Rodgers
Mary Addonizio
Mary Clarke
Mary Ann Dulcich
Mary Tinebinal
Matt Davies
Matthew Cooke
Matthew Crawford
Matthew Crossan
Matthew Eatough
Matthew Francis
Matthew Lowe
Matthew Woodman
Matthias Rosenberg
Maxwell Mankoff
Meaghan Delahunt
Meg Lovelock
Megan Wittling
Mel Pryor
Melissa Quignon-Finch
Michael Aguilar
Michael Bichko
Michael Boog
Michael Eades
Michael James Eastwood
Michael Gavin
Michael Parsons
Michaela Anchan
Michele Whitfeld
Michelle Mercaldo
Michelle Mirabella
Miguel Head
Mike Abram
Mike Barrie
Mike James
Mike Schneider
Miles Smith-Morris
Mim Lucy
Mohamed Tonsy
Molly Foster
Molly Schneider
Mona Arshi
Monica Tanouye
Morayma Jimenez
Morgan Lyons
Moriah Haefner
Myza Gouthro
Nancy Chen
Nancy Cohen
Nancy Jacobson
Nancy Oakes
Naomi Morauf
Nasiera Foflonker
Natalie Middleton
Nathalia Robbins-Cherry
Nathalie Teitler
Nathan McNamara
Nathan Weida
Nichola Smalley
Nicholas Brown
Nicholas Rutherford
Nick James
Nick Marshall
Nick Nelson & Rachel Eley
Nick Sidwell
Nick Twemlow
Nick Rushworth
Nico Parfitt
Nicola Hart
Nicolas Sampson
Nicole Matteini
Niharika Jain
Niki Sammut
Nina Aron
Nina Todorova
Norman Batchelor
Odilia Corneth
Ohan Hominis
Owen Williams
Pamela Ritchie
Pankaj Mishra
Pat Winslow
Patrick Hawley
Patrick Hoare
Patrick Liptak
Patrick Pagni
Paul Bangert
Paul Cray
Paul Ewing
Paul Gibson
Paul Jones
Paul Jordan
Paul Milhofer
Paul Munday
Paul Myatt
Paul Nightingale
Paul Scott
Paul Segal
Paul Stuart
Paul Tran-Hoang
Paula McGrath
Paula Melendez
Pavlos Stavropoulos
Pawel Szeliga
Pedro Ponce
Penelope Hewett Brown
Penelope Hewett-Brown
Pete Clough
Pete Keeley
Peter Goulborn
Peter Hayden
Peter Rowland
Peter Wells
Petra Hendrickson
Petra Stapp
Phelipe Souza Amorin
Philip Herbert
Philip Leichauer
Philip Warren
Phillipa Clements
Phillipa Milne
Phoebe McKenzie
Phoebe Millerwhite
Phyllis Reeve
Piet Van Bockstal
Rachael de Moravia
Rachael Williams
Rachel Beddow
Rachel Belt
Rachel Gaughan

Rachel Rothe
Rachel Van Riel
Rahul Kanakia
Rajni Aldridge
Ralph Jacobowitz
Rebecca Caldwell
Rebecca Maddox
Rebecca Marriott
Rebecca Michel
Rebecca Milne
Rebecca Moss
Rebecca Peer
Rebecca Rushforth
Rebecca Servadio
Rebecca Shaak
Rebecca Surin
Rebekah Lattin-Rawstrone
Renee Thomas
Rhea Pokorny
Rich Sutherland
Richard Clesham
Richard Ellis
Richard Ley-Hamilton
Richard Mansell
Richard Smith
Richard Soundy
Richard Stubbings
Richard Village
Risheeta Joshi
Rishi Dastidar
Rita Kaar
Rita Marrinson
Rita O'Brien
Robbie Matlock
Robert Gillett
Robert Sliman
Roberto Hull
Robin McLean
Robin Taylor
Robina Frank
Roger Ramsden
Ronan O'Shea
Rory Williamson
Rosabella Reeves
Rosalind May
Rosalind Ramsay
Rosemary Horsewood
Ross Beaton
Royston Tester
Roz Simpson
Ruth Curry
Ryan Day
Ryan Pierce
Sabine Griffiths
Sally Ayhan
Sally Baker
Sally Warner
Sam Gordon
Samuel Crosby
Sara Kittleson
Sara Unwin
Sarah Arboleda
Sarah Brewer
Sarah Lucas
Sasha Dugdale
Satyam Makoieva
Scott Adams
Scott Baxter
Scott Chiddister
Sean Johnston
Sean Kottke
Sean McGivern
Sean Myers
Selina Guinness
Severijn Hagemeijer
Shamala Gallagher
Shannon Knapp
Sharon Levy
Sharon Rhodes
Sharon White Gilson
Sienna Kang
Silje Bergum Kinsten
Simak Ali
Simon James
Simon Pitney
Simon Robertson
Simone Martelossi
S K Grout
Sophie Nappert
Stacy Rodgers
Stefano Mula
Stella Rieck
Stephan Eggum
Stephanie Miller
Stephanie Smee
Stephanie Wasek
Stephen Fuller
Stephen Pearsall
Stephen Wilson
Stephen Yates
Steve Chapman
Steve Clough
Steve Dearden
Steven Diggin
Steven Hess
Steven Norton
Steven Williams
Stewart Eastham
Stuart Allen
Stuart Wilkinson
Sujani Reddy
Summer Migliori Soto
Susan Edsall
Susan Jaken
Susan Morgan
Susan Winter
Susan Wachowski
Suzanne Kirkham
Suzanne Wiggins
Tania Hershman
Tania Marlowe
Tara Roman
Tatjana Soli
Tatyana Reshetnik
Taylor Ball
Terry Bone
Tess Lewis
Tessa Lang
Theo Voortman
Theresa Kelsay
Thomas Alt
Thomas Campbell
Thomas Noone
Thomas van den Bout
Thuy Dinh
Tiffany Lehr
Timothy Baker
Tina Juul Møller
Toby Ryan
Tom Darby
Tom Doyle
Tom Franklin
Tom Gray
Tom Stafford
Tom Whatmore
Tracy Northup
Trevor Latimer
Trevor Wald
Trevor Brent Marta Berto
Tulta Behm
Tyler Giesen
Val& Tom Flechtner
Valerie Carroll
Vanessa Heggie
Vanessa Nolan
Veronica Barnsley
Victor Meadowcroft
Victoria Goodbody
Vijay Pattisapu
Vilma Nikolaidou
Wendy Langridge
William Brockenborough
William Mackenzie
William Schwaber
William Wilson
William Orton
Yoora Yi Tenen
Zachary Maricondia